Barefoot
in the Park

A COMEDY IN THREE ACTS

By Neil Simon

SAMUEL FRENCH, INC.
45 WEST 25TH STREET   NEW YORK 10001
7623 SUNSET BOULEVARD   HOLLYWOOD 90046
LONDON   *TORONTO*

BAREFOOT IN THE PARK, by Neil Simon, directed by Mike Nichols, was presented by Saint Subber at the Biltmore Theatre, N.Y.C., Oct. 23, 1963.

CAST OF CHARACTERS

CORIE BRATTER ....*Elizabeth Ashley*

TELEPHONE REPAIR MAN ....*Herbert Edelman*

DELIVERY MAN ....*Joseph Keating*

PAUL BRATTER ....*Robert Redford*

CORIE'S MOTHER, MRS. BANKS ....*Mildred Natwick*

VICTOR VELASCO ....*Kurt Kaznar*

SYNOPSIS OF SCENES

ACT ONE

The top floor of a brownstone on East 48th Street, New York City. About 5:30 on a cold February afternoon.

ACT TWO

SCENE 1: Four days later. About 7:00 P.M.

SCENE 2: Later that night. About 2 A.M.

ACT THREE

The following day. About 5:00 P.M.

Barefoot in the Park

ACT I

SCENE: *A large one-room apartment on the top floor of an old brownstone in the East Forties off Third Avenue. The room is barren. A ladder, canvas drop cloth, and a couple of empty paint cans stand forlornly in the center of the room. There is a huge skylight which pours the bright February SUNSHINE glaringly into the room. Through the skylight we can see the roofs and windows of brownstones across the street and the framework of a large building under construction. Crests of clinging snow can be seen in the two windows under the skylight. At Stage Right, there is the entrance door, a step below the apartment itself. At Stage Left, four steps lead to a raised area from which two doors open, the Upstage one leading to a bathroom, the Left one to the bedroom. Although we can't see much of the latter, we will soon learn that it isn't really a bedroom. It's a dressing room, about 6' x 4'. The bathroom has no tub. Just a shower and a sink and what have you. On another raised section Up Right is the kitchen. It's not really a kitchen. It's just an old stove, an older refrigerator and a chipped sink that stands nakedly between them. Upstage Left of this area is another platform on which stand a steamer trunk and a few suitcases. The room has just been freshly painted. Not carefully, maybe not professionally, but painted. There is a small Franklin Stove Downstage Left below the platform, and an open closet Downstage Right. Completing the furnishings of the room are a railing that runs Downstage of the entrance wall, and a radiator that sits high on the Upstage Left wall. For all the room's drabness and coldness, there*

5

is great promise here. Someone with taste, imagination and personality can make this that perfect love nest we all dream about.

At Rise: *That person is now putting the key in the door. It opens and* CORIE BRATTER *enters. She is lovely, young and full of hope for the future. She enters the apartment, looks around and sighs as though the world were just beginning. For her, it is. She is wearing levis and a yellow top under a large, shaggy white fur coat. She carries a bouquet of flowers. After rapturously examining the room, she takes the small paint can, fills it with water and puts in the flowers, throwing the wrapping on the floor. The first bit of color in the room. As she crosses to put the "vase" on top of the Franklin Stove Down Left, the* DOORBELL *buzzes. After putting the flowers down, she crosses to the door, buzzes back, and then opens the door and shouts down:*

CORIE. Hello?

(*From the depths, possibly from the bottom of the earth, we hear a VOICE shout up.*)

VOICE. Bratter?
CORIE. (*Yelling back.*) Yes. Up here! . . . Top floor! (*She crosses to the suitcases, opens the medium-sized one and takes out a large bottle of champagne which she puts into the refrigerator.*)

(*From below, the VOICE again, this time a little closer.*)

VOICE. Hello?

(CORIE *rushes to the door again and shouts down.*)

CORIE. Up here! You have another floor to go.

(*Crossing back to the open suitcase she takes out three*

*small logs and carries them to the stove. As she
drops them in front of the stove, the voice appears
at the door. A tall, heavy-set* MAN *in his mid-thir-
ties, in a plaid wool jacket and baseball cap and
breathing very, very hard.*)

MAN. Tel— (*He tries to catch his breath.*) Telephone
Company.
CORIE. Oh, the phone. Good. Come on in.

(*He steps in, carrying a black leather repair kit.*)

MAN. That's quite a— (*Breath, breath.*) quite a climb.
CORIE. Yes, it's five flights. If you don't count the
front stoop.
MAN. I *counted* the front stoop. (*Breath, breath. He
looks at his notebook.*) Paul Bratter, right?
CORIE. *Mrs.* Paul Bratter.
MAN. (*Still checking book.*) Princess phone?
CORIE. The little one? That lights up? In beige?
MAN. The little one. . . . (*Breath, breath.*) That lights
up. . . . (*Breath, breath.*) In beige. . . . (*Breath, breath.
Swallows hard.*)
CORIE. Would you like a glass of water?
MAN. (*Sucking for air, nods.*) Please!
CORIE. (*Crosses to sink.*) I'd offer you soda or a beer
but we don't have anything yet.
MAN. A glass of water's fine.
CORIE. (*Suddenly embarrassed.*) . . . Expect I don't
have a glass either.
MAN. Oh!
CORIE. Nothing's arrived yet . . . You could put your
head under and just schlurp.
MAN. No, I'm okay. Just a little out of shape. (*As he
stiffly climbs up the step out of the well, he groans with
pain. After looking about.*) Where do you want the
phone?
CORIE. (*Looks around.*) The phone . . . Let me see
. . . Gee, I don't know. Do you have any ideas?

MAN. Well, it depends what you're gonna do with the room. You gonna have furniture in here?

CORIE. Yes, it's on its way up.

MAN. (*He looks back at the stairs.*) *Heavy* furniture?

CORIE. I'll tell you what. (*She points to telephone junction box on the wall* D. L. *of the stairs to the bedroom.*) Just put it over there and give me a long extension cord. If I can't find a place, I'll just hang it out the window.

MAN. Fair enough. (*He crosses to the junction box, coughing and in pain.*) Whoo!

CORIE. Say, I'm awfully sorry about the stairs. (*Taking the large suitcase, she starts to drag it into the bedroom.*)

MAN. (*On his knees, opens tool box.*) You're really gonna live up here, heh? . . . I mean, every day?

CORIE. Every day.

MAN. You don't mind it?

CORIE. (*Stopping on the stairs.*) Mind it . . . ? I love this apartment . . . (*Continues into bedroom.*) Well, it *does* discourage people.

MAN. What people?

CORIE. (*Comes out of bedroom and starts for other suitcases.*) Mothers, friends, relatives, mothers. I mean no one just "pops" in on you when they have to climb five flights.

MAN. You're a newlywed, right?

CORIE. Six days. What gave me away?

MAN. I watch "What's My Line" a lot.

(*The DOORBELL buzzes.*)

CORIE. OH! I hope that's the furniture.

MAN. I don't want to see this.

CORIE. (*Presses buzzer and yells down the stairs.*) Helloooo! Bloomingdale's?

(*From below, a* VOICE.)

VOICE. Lord and Taylor.

CORIE. Lord and Taylor? (*Shrugs and takes the now-empty suitcase and puts it into the closet* D. R.) Probably another wedding gift . . . From my mother. She sends me wedding gifts twice a day . . .

MAN. I hope it's an electric heater. (*He blows on his hands.*)

CORIE. (*Worried, she feels the steam pipe next to the closet.*) Really? Is it cold in here?

MAN. I can't grip the screw driver. Maybe the steam is off.

CORIE. Maybe that's it. (*She gets up on stairs and tests the radiator.*)

MAN. Just turn it on. It'll come right up.

CORIE. It *is* on. It's just not coming up.

MAN. Oh! . . . Well, that's these old brownstones for you. (*Zips up his jacket.*)

CORIE. I prefer it this way. It's a medical fact, you know, that steam is very bad for you.

MAN. Yeah? In February?

(*Suddenly the Lord and Taylor* DELIVERY MAN *appears in the door, carrying three packages. He is in his early sixties and from the way he is breathing, it seems the end is very near. He gasps for air.*)

CORIE. (*Crossing to him.*) Oh, hi . . . Just put it down . . . anywhere. (*The* DELIVERY MAN *puts the packages down, panting. He wants to talk but can't. He extends his hand to the* TELEPHONE MAN *for a bit of compassion.*)

MAN. I know. I know.

CORIE. I'm awfully sorry about the stairs. (*The* DELIVERY MAN *takes out a pad and pencil and holds them out limply towards* CORIE.) What's this?

MAN. I think he wants you to sign it.

CORIE. Oh, yes. (*She signs it quickly.*) Wait, just a minute. (*She picks up her bag from where she had left it in the kitchen area and takes out some change.*) Here you go . . . (*She puts it in his hand. He nods weakly and turns to go.*) Will you be all right . . . ? (*And for*

*the first time he gets out some words. They are . . .
"Argh, argh." He exits. Closes door behind him.*) It's a
shame, isn't it? Giving such hard work to an old man.
(*Takes two of the packages and places them Upstage
with the remaining suitcases.*)

MAN. He's probably only 25. They age fast on this
route. (*He dials. Into phone.*) Hello, Ed? Yeah . . . On
. . . er . . . Eldorado 5-8191 . . . Give me a straight
check.

CORIE. (*Moving to* TELEPHONE MAN.) Is that my
number? Eldorado 5-8191? (MAN *nods.*) It has a nice
sound, hasn't it?

MAN. (*Why fool with a romantic.*) Yeah, it's a beautiful number. (*The PHONE rings, He answers it—dis-
guising his voice.*) Hello? . . . (*Chuckles over his joke.*)
Good work, Mr. Bell, you've done it again. (*He hangs
up, turns to* CORIE.) Well, you've got your phone. As
my mother would say, may your first call be from the
Sweepstakes.

CORIE. (*Takes phone.*) My very own phone . . . Gives
you a sense of power, doesn't it Can I make a call yet?

MAN. (*Putting cover back on junction box.*) Your bill
started two minutes ago.

CORIE. Who can I call? . . . I know. (*She starts to
dial.*)

MAN. Oh, by the way. My name is Harry Pepper. And
if you ever have any trouble with this phone, please, do
me a favor, don't ask for Harry Pepper. (CORIE *hangs up,
a look of disappointment on her face.*) What's the matter,
bad news?

CORIE. (*Like a telephone operator.*) It is going to be
cloudy tonight with a light snow.

MAN. (*He looks up at skylight.*) And just think, you'll
be the first one in the city to see it fall.

(*The DOORBELL buzzes.* CORIE *puts down the phone,
and rushes to the door.*)

CORIE. Oh, please, let that be the furniture and not

Paul so Paul can see the apartment with furniture. (*She buzzes, opens door and yells downstairs.*) Yes?

VOICE FROM BELOW. It's me!

CORIE. (*Unhappily.*) Oh, hi, Paul. (*She turns into room.*) Well, I guess he sees the apartment without the furniture. (*Takes remaining package and places it with others on landing under the windows.*)

MAN. (*Gathering up his tools.*) How long d'ja say you were married?

CORIE. Six days.

MAN. He won't notice the place is empty until June. (*He crosses to door.*) Well, Eldorado 5-8191 . . . Have a nice marriage . . . (*Turns back into room.*) And may you soon have many extensions. (*He turns and looks at the climb down he has to make and moans.*) Ooohh! (*He is gone.*)

(CORIE *quickly starts to prepare the room for* PAUL'S *initial entrance. She gathers up the canvas drop cloth and throws it into the closet.*)

PAUL'S VOICE. Corie? . . . Where are you?

CORIE. (*Rushes back to door and yells down.*) Up here, hon . . . Top floor . . . (*The PHONE rings.*) Oh, my goodness. The phone. (*She rushes to it and answers it.*) Hello? . . . Yes? . . . Oh, yes, he is . . . I mean he's on his way up . . . Can you hold on for two more floors? (*She puts down receiver and yells.*) Paul. Hurry up, darling!

PAUL'S VOICE. Okay. Okay.

CORIE. (*Into phone.*) Hello. He'll be with you in one more flight. Thank you. (*She puts phone on floor and continues to get the apartment ready. Rushing up the stairs she closes the bedroom and the bathroom doors. Surveying the room, she sees the wrapping from the flowers on the floor of the kitchen and the wadded-up newspapers on top of the stove. Quickly gathering them up, she stuffs them into the nearest hiding place, the refrigerator. Then dashing into the hall and closing the door behind her, she re-enters to make one more survey of her apartment. Satisfied with what she sees, she turns back to the open door, and yells down.*) Now honey, don't expect too much. The furniture didn't get here yet and the paint didn't come out exactly right, but I think it's going to be beautiful . . . Paul? . . . Paul, are you all right?

PAUL'S VOICE. I'm coming. I'm coming.

CORIE. (*Into phone.*) He's coming. He's coming. (*She puts down phone and looks at door. PAUL falls in through doorway and hangs on the rail at the entrance of the apartment. PAUL is 26 but breathes and dresses like 56. He carries a heavy suitcase and an attaché case and all the dignity he can bear. He drops the attaché case at the railing.*) Hi, sweetheart. (*She smothers him with kisses but all he can do is fight for air.*) Oh, Paul, darling. (*He sucks for oxygen.*) Well? (*She steps back.*) Say something.

PAUL. (*Breathing with great difficulty, looks back down the stairs.*) It's six flights . . . Did you know it's six flights?

CORIE. It isn't. It's five.

PAUL. (*Staggers up the step into the room, and collapses on the suitcase.*) What about that big thing hanging outside the building?

CORIE. That's not a flight. It's a stoop.

PAUL. It may *look* like a stoop but it climbs like a flight. (*Breath, breath.*)

CORIE. Is that *all* you have to say?

PAUL. (*Gasping.*) I didn't think I'd get that much out. (*He breathes heavily.*) It didn't seem like six flights when I first saw the apartment. (*Breath.*) Why is that?

CORIE. You didn't see the apartment. Don't you remember, the woman wasn't home. You saw the third floor apartment.

PAUL. Then that's why.

CORIE. (*Crossing above PAUL.*) You don't like it. You really don't like it.

PAUL. I *do* like it. (*He squints around.*) I'm just waiting for my eyes to clear first.

CORIE. I expected you to walk in here and say, "Wow." (*Takes his hand.*)

PAUL. I will. (*He takes a deep breath.*) Okay. (*He looks around, then says without enthusiasm.*) "Wow."

CORIE. Oh, Paul. (*She throws herself onto* PAUL's *knee.*) It'll be beautiful, I promise you. You just came home too soon. (*Nuzzles* PAUL.)

PAUL. You know I missed you.

CORIE. Did you really?

PAUL. Right in the middle of the Monday morning conference I began to feel sexy.

CORIE. That's marvelous. (*They kiss.*) Oh, boy. Let's take a cab back to the Plaza. We still have an hour before check-out time.

PAUL. We can't. We took a towel and two ash trays. We're hot. (*He kisses her.*)

CORIE. My gosh, you still love me.

PAUL. After six days at the Plaza? What's the trick?

CORIE. (*Gets up and moves away.*) But that was a honeymoon. Now we're on a regular schedule. I thought you'd come home tonight, and we'd shake hands and start the marriage. (*She extends her hand to him.*)

PAUL. (*Rises.*) "How do you do . . . ?"

(*They shake hands. Then* CORIE *throws herself into his arms and kisses him.*)

CORIE. My turn to say "Wow" . . . For a lawyer you're some good kisser.

PAUL. (*With hidden import.*) For a kisser I'm some good lawyer.

CORIE. What does that mean? . . . Something's happened? . . . Something wonderful? . . . Well, for pete's sakes, what?

PAUL. It's not positive yet. The office is supposed to call and let me know in five minutes.

CORIE. (*Then she remembers.*) Oh! They called!

PAUL. What—?

CORIE. I mean they're calling.

PAUL. When—?

CORIE. Now— They're on the phone now.

PAUL. (*Looking around.*) Where—?

CORIE. (*Points to phone.*) There—

PAUL. (*Rushes to phone.*) Why didn't you tell me?

CORIE. I forgot. You kissed me and got me all crazy.

PAUL. (*Into phone.*) Frank? . . . Yeah! . . . Listen, what did— Oh, very funny. (*Looks to* CORIE.) "For a lawyer, I'm some good kisser" . . . Come on, come, tell me . . . Well? . . . (*A big grin.* CORIE *feeling left out, sneaks over and tries to tickle him.*) You're kidding? The whole thing? Oh, Frank, baby. I love you . . . What do you mean, nervous? . . . I passed the bar, didn't I? . . . Yes, I'll go over everything tonight. (CORIE *reacts to "tonight" and slowly moves to the ladder.*) I'll meet you in Schraffts at eight o'clock in the morning. We'll go over the briefs . . . Hey, what kind of a tie do I wear? I don't know. I thought maybe something flowing like Oliver Wendell Holmes' . . . Right. (*He stands up. He is bubbling with joy.* CORIE *has now climbed up the ladder.*) Did you hear? . . . Did you hear? (*Moves up ladder to* CORIE.)

CORIE. What about tonight?

PAUL. I've got to be in court tomorrow morning . . . *I've got my first case!*

CORIE. What about tonight?

PAUL. I'll have to go over the briefs. Marshall has to be in Washington tomorrow and he wants me to take over . . . with Frank . . . but it's really my case. (*He hugs* CORIE.) Oh, Corie, baby, I'm going to be a lawyer.

CORIE. That's wonderful . . . I just thought we were going to spend tonight together.

PAUL. We'll spend tomorrow night together. (*Crosses to railing and gets attaché case.*) I hope I brought those affidavits.

CORIE. *I* brought a black nightgown. (*She crosses up to small suitcase.*)

PAUL. (*Looking through affidavits from case; his mind has now turned completely legal.*) Marshall had everything laid out when I was at the office . . . It looks simple enough. A furrier is suing a woman for non-payment of bills.

CORIE. (*Taking nightgown out of suitcase.*) I was going to cook you spaghetti with the white clam sauce . . . in a bikini.

PAUL. We're representing the furrier. He made four specially tailored coats for this woman on Park Avenue. Now she doesn't want the coats.

CORIE. (*Takes off blouse, and slipping her arms through the nightgown straps, she drapes it over her.*) Then I found this great thing on Eighth Street. It's a crossword puzzle with dirty words.

PAUL. But the furrier can't get rid of the coats. She's only four foot eight. He'd have to sell them to a rich little girl.

CORIE. Then I was going to put on a record and do an authentic Cambodian fertility dance.

PAUL. The only trouble is, he didn't have a signed contract . . . (CORIE *begins her "fertility dance" and ends up collapsing on the bottom step of the ladder.*) What are you doing?

CORIE. I'm trying to get you all hot and bothered and you're summing up for the jury. The whole marriage is over.

PAUL. (*Moves to* CORIE.) Oh, Corie, honey, I'm sorry. (*Puts his arms around her.*) I guess I'm pretty excited. You want me to be rich and famous, don't you?

CORIE. During the day. At night I want you to be here and sexy.

PAUL. I will. Just as soon as "Birnbaum versus Gump" is over . . . I'll tell you what. Tomorrow night is your night. We'll do whatever you want.

CORIE. Something wild, insane and crazy?

PAUL. I promise.

CORIE. (*Eyes wide open.*) Like what?

PAUL. Well . . . I'll come home early and we'll wall-paper each other.

CORIE. Oh, Paul, how wonderful . . . Can't we do it tonight?

PAUL. No, we can't do it tonight, because tonight I've got to work. (*Rises, and looks around.*) Except where do I sit?

CORIE. The furniture will be here by five. They promised.

PAUL. (*Dropping affidavits into case, looks at his watch.*) Five? . . . It's five-thirty. (*Crosses to bedroom stairs.*) What do we do, sleep in Bloomingdale's tonight?

CORIE. They'll be here, Paul. They're probably stuck in traffic.

PAUL. (*Crossing up to bedroom.*) And what about tonight? I've got a case in court tomorrow. Maybe we should check into a hotel? (*Looks into bedroom.*)

CORIE. (*Rises and moves towards* PAUL.) We just checked *out* of a hotel. I don't care if the furniture *doesn't* come. I'm sleeping in my apartment *tonight.*

PAUL. Where? Where? (*Looks into bathroom, closes door, and starts to come back down the steps.*) There's only room for one in the bathtub. (*He suddenly turns, goes back up steps and opens door to the bathroom.*) Where's the bathtub?

CORIE. (*Hesitantly.*) There is no bathtub.

PAUL. No bathtub?

CORIE. There's a shower . . .

PAUL. How am I going to take a bath?

CORIE. You won't take a bath. You'll take a shower.

PAUL. I don't like showers. I like baths. Corie, how am I going to take a bath?

CORIE. You'll lie down in the shower and hang your feet over the sink. . . . I'm sorry there's no bathtub, Paul.

PAUL. (*Closes door, and crosses down into room.*) Hmmmm . . . Boy, of all the nights . . . (*He suddenly shivers.*) It's freezing in here. (*He rubs his hands.*) Isn't there any heat?

CORIE. Of course there's heat. We have a radiator.

PAUL. (*Gets up on steps and feels radiator.*) The *radiator's* the coldest thing in the room.

CORIE. It's probably the boiler. It's probably off in the whole building.

PAUL. (*Putting on gloves.*) No, it was warm coming up the stairs. (*Goes out door into hall.*) See. . . . It's nice and warm out here.

CORIE. Maybe it's because the apartment is empty.

PAUL. The *hall* is empty too but it's warm out here.

CORIE. (*Moves to the stove.*) It'll be all right once I get a fire going.

PAUL. (*Goes to phone.*) A fire? You'd have to keep the flame going night and day . . . I'll call the landlord.

CORIE. (*Putting log into stove.*) He's not home.

PAUL. Where is he?

CORIE. In Florida! . . . There's a handy man that comes Mondays, Wednesdays, and Fridays.

PAUL. You mean we freeze on Tuesdays, Thursdays and Saturdays?

CORIE. He'll be here in the morning.

PAUL. (*Moving R.*) And what'll we do tonight? I've got a case in court in the morning.

CORIE. (*Moves to PAUL.*) Will you stop saying it like you always have a case in court in the morning. This is your first one.

PAUL. Well, what'll we do?

CORIE. The furniture will be here. In the meantime I can light the stove and you can sit over the fire with your law books and a shawl like Abraham Lincoln. (*Crosses to the Franklin Stove and gets matches from the top of the stove.*)

PAUL. Is that supposed to be funny? (*Begins to investigate small windows.*)

CORIE. No. It was supposed to be nasty. It just came out funny. (*She strikes match and attempts to light the log in stove. PAUL tries the windows.*) What are you doing? (*Givs up attempting to light log.*)

PAUL. I'm checking to see if the windows are closed.

CORIE. They're closed. I looked.

PAUL. Then why is it windy in here?

CORIE. (*Moves* R. *to* PAUL.) I don't feel a draft.

PAUL. (*Moves away from windows.*) I didn't say draft. I said wind . . . There's a brisk, northeasterly wind blowing in this room.

CORIE. You don't have to get sarcastic.

PAUL. (*Moving up into the kitchen area.*) I'm not getting sarcastic, I'm getting chapped lips. (*Looking up, he glimpses the hole in the skylight.*)

CORIE. How could there be wind in a closed room?

PAUL. How's this for an answer? There's a hole in the skylight. (*He points up.*)

CORIE. (*She looks up, sees it and is obviously embarrassed by it.*) Gee, I didn't see that before. Did you?

PAUL. (*Moves to ladder.*) I didn't see the *apartment* before.

CORIE. (*Defensively. Crosses to the railing and gets her coat.*) All right, Paul, don't get upset. I'm sure it'll be fixed. We could plug it up with something for tonight.

PAUL. (*Gets up on ladder.*) How? How? That's twenty feet high. You'd have to fly over in a plane and *drop* something in.

CORIE. (*Putting on coat.*) It's only for one night. And it's not that cold.

PAUL. In February? Do you know what it's like at three o'clock in the morning? In February? Ice-cold freezing.

CORIE. It's not going to be freezing. I called the weather bureau. It's going to be cloudy with a light s— (*She catches herself and looks up.*)

PAUL. What? (CORIE *turns away.*) What? . . . A light what?

CORIE. Snow!

PAUL. (*Coming down ladder.*) *Snow??* . . . It's going to snow tonight? . . . In here?

CORIE. They're wrong as often as they're right.

PAUL. I'm going to be shoveling snow in my own living room.

CORIE. It's a little hole.

PAUL. With that wind it could blow six-foot drifts in the bathroom. Honestly, Corie, I don't see how you can be so calm about all this.

CORIE. Well, what is it you want me to do?

PAUL. Go to pieces, like me. It's only natural.

CORIE. (*Goes to him and puts her arms around him.*) I've got a better idea. I'll keep you warm . . . And there's no charge for electricity . . . (*Kisses him.*)

PAUL. I can see I haven't got much of a law career ahead of me.

CORIE. Good. I hope we starve. And they find us up here dead in each other's arms.

PAUL. "Frozen skinny lovers found on 48th Street." (*They kiss.*)

CORIE. Are we in love again?

PAUL. We're in love again. (*They kiss again, a long passionate embrace.*)

(*The DOORBELL buzzes.*)

CORIE. (*Breaking away.*) The bed. I hope it's the bed. (*She buzzes back, and then opens door and yells down.*) Helllooooo! Bloomingdale's?

FEMALE VOICE. (*From below.*) Surprise!

CORIE. (*Turns to* PAUL.) Oh, God.

PAUL. What's wrong?

CORIE. Please, let it be a woman delivering the furniture.

PAUL. A woman?

VOICE. Corie?

CORIE. But it's my mother.

PAUL. Your mother? Now?

CORIE. (*Taking nightgown off and slipping into blouse.*) She couldn't wait. Just one more day.

PAUL. (*Puts affidavits back into case.*) Corie, you've got to get rid of her. I've got a case in court tomorrow.

CORIE. It's ugly in here without furniture, isn't it? She's just going to hate it, won't she?

VOICE. Corie? Where are you?

CORIE. (*Crosses to door and yells down stairs.*) Up here, Mom. Top floor.

PAUL. (*Hides case in corner L. of windows.*) How am I going to work tonight?

CORIE. She'll think this is the way we're going to live. Like gypsies in an empty store. (*Attempting to button top.*)

PAUL. (*Throwing nightgown and lingerie into suitcase.*) Maybe I ought to sleep in the office.

CORIE. She'll freeze to death. She'll sit there in her fur coat and freeze to death.

PAUL. (*Helps her button top.*) I don't get you, Corie. Five minutes ago this was the Garden of Eden. Now it's suddenly Cannery Row.

CORIE. She doesn't understand, Paul. She has a different set of values. She's practical. She's not young like us.

PAUL. (*Gathers up suitcase with lingerie and takes it into bedroom.*) Well, I'm 26 and cold as hell.

VOICE. (*Getting nearer.*) Corie?

CORIE. (*Yells down at door.*) One more flight, Mother . . . Paul, promise me one thing. Don't tell her about the rent. If she asks, tell her you're not quite sure yet.

PAUL. (*Crossing to door with coat collar up around his face.*) Not sure what my rent is? I *have* to know what my rent is. I'm a college graduate.

CORIE. (*Stopping PAUL.*) Can't you lie a little? For Me? You don't have to tell her it's a hundred and twenty-five.

PAUL. All right. How much is it?

CORIE. Sixty?

PAUL. What?

CORIE. Sixty-five?

PAUL. Corie—

CORIE. Seventy-five, all right? Seventy-five dollars and sixty-three cents a month. Including gas and electricity. She'll believe that, won't she?

PAUL. *Anyone* would believe that. It's the hundred and twenty-five that's hard to swallow. (*Combs hair.*)

CORIE. She's taking a long time. I hope she's all right.

PAUL. I can't lie about the stairs. She's going to figure out it's six floors all by herself.

CORIE. Shh. Shh, she's here. (*Starts to open door.*)

PAUL. (*Grabs her.*) Just promise *me* one thing. Don't let her stay too long because I've got a—

CORIE. (*With him.*) —case in court in the morning . . . I know, I know . . . (*She opens door and goes into hall.*) Mother!

(*The* MOTHER *shoots by her into the room and grabs the rail to keep from falling. She's in her late forties, pretty, but has not bothered to look after herself these past few years. She could use a permanent and a whole new wardrobe.*)

PAUL. (*Rushes to support her.*) Hello, Mom.

(*The* MOTHER *struggles for air.*)

MOTHER. Oh! . . . Oh! . . . I can't breathe.

CORIE. Take it easy, Mom. (*Holding her other arm.*)

MOTHER. I can't catch my breath.

PAUL. You should have rested.

MOTHER. I did . . . But there were always more stairs.

CORIE. Paul, help her.

PAUL. Come on, Mom. Watch the step. (*Starts to lead her up the step into the room.*)

MOTHER. More stairs? (*She steps up.*)

(CORIE *and* PAUL *lead* MOTHER *towards* PAUL's *suitcase, still standing near the wall.*)

CORIE. You want some water?

MOTHER. Later. I can't swallow yet.

PAUL. Here, sit down.

(*She sits on suitcase.*)

MOTHER. Oh, my.

CORIE. It's not *that* high, Mother.

MOTHER. I know, dear. It's not bad really . . . What is it, nine flights?

PAUL. Five. We don't count the stoop.

MOTHER. I didn't think I'd make it . . . If I'd known the people on the third floor I'd have gone to visit them . . .

(PAUL *sits on the bottom step of the ladder.*)

CORIE. This is a pleasant surprise, Mother.

MOTHER. Well, I really had no intention of coming up, but I had a luncheon in Westchester and I thought, since it's on my way home, I might as well drop in for a few minutes . . .

CORIE. On your way home to New Jersey?

MOTHER. Yes. I just came over the Whitestone Bridge and down the Major Deegan Highway and now I'll cut across town and on to the Henry Hudson Parkway and up to the George Washington Bridge. It's no extra trouble.

PAUL. Sounds easy enough.

MOTHER. Yes . . .

CORIE. We were going to ask you over on Friday.

MOTHER. Friday. Good. I'll be here Friday . . . I'm not going to stay now, I know you both must be busy.

PAUL. Well, as a matter of fact—

CORIE. (*Stopping him.*) No, we're not, are we, Paul?

(*He kills her with a glance.*)

MOTHER. Besides, Aunt Harriet is ringing the bell for me in ten minutes . . . Just one good look around, that's all. I'm not sure I'm coming back.

CORIE. I wish you could have come an hour later. After the furniture arrived.

MOTHER. (*Gets up, looks and stops cold.*) Don't worry. I've got a marvelous imagination.

CORIE. Well . . . ?

MOTHER. (*Stunned.*) Oh, Corie . . . it's . . . beautiful.

CORIE. You hate it . . .

MOTHER. (*Moves up towards windows.*) No, no . . . It's a charming apartment. (*Trips over platform.*) I love it.

CORIE. (*Rushes to her.*) You can't really tell like this.

MOTHER. I'm crazy about it.

CORIE. It's not your kind of apartment. I knew you wouldn't like it.

MOTHER. (*Moves down to* PAUL.) I love it . . . Paul, didn't I say I loved it? (*Takes his hand.*)

PAUL. She said she loved it.

MOTHER. I knew I said it.

CORIE. (*To* MOTHER.) Do you really, Mother? I mean are you absolutely crazy in love with it?

MOTHER. Oh, yes. It's very cute . . . And there's so much you can do with it.

CORIE. I told you she hated it.

MOTHER. (*Moves towards bedroom landing.*) Corie, you don't give a person a chance. At least let me see the whole apartment.

PAUL. . . . This *is* the whole apartment.

MOTHER. (*Cheerfully.*) It's a nice, large room.

CORIE. There's a bedroom.

MOTHER. Where?

PAUL. One flight up.

CORIE. It's four little steps. (*Goes up steps to bedroom door.*) See. One-two-three-four.

MOTHER. (*To* PAUL.) Oh. Split level. (*Climbs steps.*) And where's the bedroom? Through there?

CORIE. No. *In* there. That's the bedroom . . . It's really just a dressing room but I'm going to use it as a bedroom.

MOTHER. (*At bedroom door.*) That's a wonderful idea. And you can just put a bed in there.

CORIE. That's right.

MOTHER. How?

(PAUL *moves to the steps.*)

CORIE. It'll fit. I measured the room.

MOTHER. A double bed?

CORIE. No, an oversized single.

MOTHER. Oh, they're nice. And where will Paul sleep?

CORIE. With me.'

PAUL. (*Moves up on landing.*) In an oversized single?

MOTHER. I'm sure you'll be comfortable.

CORIE. I'm positive.

(PAUL *moves back down stairs and glumly surveys the room.*)

MOTHER. It's a wonderful idea. Very clever . . .

CORIE. Thank you.

MOTHER. Except you can't get to the closet.

CORIE. Yes you can.

MOTHER. Without climbing over the bed?

CORIE. No, you *have* to climb over the bed.

MOTHER. That's a good idea.

CORIE. (*Leaves bedroom, crosses to ladder and climbs up.*) Everything's just temporary. As they say in McCall's, it won't really take shape until the bride's own personality becomes more clearly defined.

MOTHER. I think it's *you* right now. (*Turns to other door.*) What's in here . . . ? (*Opens door and looks in.*) The bathroom . . . (*Closes door.*) No bathtub . . . You really have quite a lot here, for one room. (*Moves down steps.*) And where's the kitchen? (*Sees stove and refrigerator, stops in horror and then crosses towards kitchen.*) Whoo, there it is . . . Very cozy. I suppose you'll eat out a lot the first year.

CORIE. We're never eating out. It's big enough to make spaghetti and things.

MOTHER. What "things"?

CORIE. It's a dish I make, called "Things." Honestly Mother, we won't starve.

MOTHER. I know, dear. (*Under skylight.*) It's chilly in here. Do you feel a draft?

PAUL. (*Looks up.*) Uh, stand over here, Mom. (*Moves her away from hole and near steam pipe next to the railing.*)

CORIE. What you need is a drink. Paul, why don't you run down and get some scotch?

PAUL. Now?

MOTHER. (*Crossing towards franklin stove.*) Oh, not for me. I'm leaving in a few minutes.

PAUL. Oh. She's leaving in a few minutes.

CORIE. She can stay for one drink.

(PAUL *quietly argues with* CORIE *at ladder.*)

MOTHER. There's so much you can do in here. Lots of wall space. What color are you going to paint it?

CORIE. It's painted.

MOTHER. Very attractive.

PAUL. (*Looks at watch.*) Wow. Nearly six.

MOTHER. I've got to go.

CORIE. Not until you have a drink . . . (*To* PAUL.) Will you get the scotch.

(*He continues to argue with her.*)

MOTHER. All right. I'll stay for just one drink.

PAUL. Good. I'll get the scotch. (*Starts for door.*)

MOTHER. Button up, dear. It's cold.

PAUL. I've noticed that.

CORIE. And get some cheese.

(PAUL *is gone.*)

MOTHER. Paul! (PAUL *reappears at the door.* MOTHER *extends her arms.*) I just want to give my fella a kiss. And wish him luck. (PAUL *comes back in and crosses all the way over to* MOTHER. *She kisses him.*) Your new home is absolutely beautiful. It's a perfect little apartment.

PAUL. Oh . . . thanks, Mom.

MOTHER. Then you *do* like it?

PAUL. Like it? (*He looks at* CORIE *and starts to exit.*) Where else can you find anything like this . . . for seventy-five sixty-three a month? (*Exits.*)

(CORIE *and* MOTHER *are alone.* CORIE *climbs down the ladder, and looks for some sign of approval from* MOTHER.)

CORIE. Well?
MOTHER. Oh, Corie, I'm so excited for you.

(They embrace.)

CORIE. It's not exactly what you pictured, is it, Mother?
MOTHER. Well, it is *unusual*—like you. (*Crosses* R.) I remember when you were a little girl you said you wanted to live on the moon. (*Turns back to* CORIE.) I thought you were joking . . . What about Paul? Is he happy with all this?
CORIE. He's happy with me. I think it's the same thing. Why?
MOTHER. I worry about you two. You're so impulsive. You jump into life. Paul is like me. He looks first. (*Sits down on suitcase.*)
CORIE. He doesn't look. He stares. That's the trouble with both of you . . . (*Places paint can next to* MOTHER *and sits.*) Oh, Mother, you don't know how I dreaded your coming up here. I was sure you'd think I was completely out of my mind.
MOTHER. Why should you think that, dear?
CORIE. Well, it's the first thing I've ever done on my own. Without your help . . .
MOTHER. If you wanted it, I'm sure you would have asked for it . . . but you didn't. And I understand.
CORIE. I hope you do, Mother. It's something I just had to do all by myself.
MOTHER. Corie, you mustn't think I'm hurt. I'm not hurt.
CORIE. I'm so glad.
MOTHER. You mustn't think I'm hurt. I don't get hurt over things like that.
CORIE. I didn't think you would.
MOTHER. *Other* things hurt me, but not that . . .

CORIE. Good . . . Hey, let's open my presents and see what I've got. And you try to act surprised. (*Gets presents and brings them down to paint can.*)

MOTHER. You won't let me buy you anything . . . Oh, they're just a few little things.

CORIE. (*Sitting down and shaking smallest box vigorously.*) What's in here. It sounds expensive.

MOTHER. Well, *now* I think it's a broken clock.

CORIE. (*Opens box, throwing wrappings and tissue paper on floor.*) I'll bet you cleaned out Saks' Gift Department. I think I'm a regular stop on the delivery route now. (*Looks at clock, puts it back in box and puts it aside and begins to open largest box.*)

MOTHER. Aunt Harriet was with me when I picked it out. (*Laughs.*) She thinks I'm over here every day now.

CORIE. You know you're welcome, Mother.

MOTHER. I said, "Why, Harriet? Just because I'm alone now," I said. "I'm not afraid to live alone. In some ways it's better to live alone," I said.

(CORIE *examines the blanket she finds in package, closes box, puts it aside and begins to open final package.* MOTHER *picks up piece of tissue paper and smooths it out on her lap.*)

MOTHER. But you can't tell her that. She thinks a woman living alone, way out in New Jersey is the worst thing in the world . . . "It's not," I told her. "It's not the *worst* thing . . ."

CORIE. (*Has package open and takes out the dismantled parts of a coffee pot.*) Hey, does this come with directions?

MOTHER. If I knew about this kitchen, it would have come with hot coffee. (*Laughs.*)

CORIE. (*Picks up box with clock and takes it with parts of coffee pot up into kitchen.*) Mother, you're an absolute angel. But you've got to stop buying things for me. It's getting embarrassing. (*Puts clock on refrigerator and coffee pot on sink.*) If you keep it up I'm going to open a discount house . . . (*Takes blanket and places it with suitcase near windows.*)

MOTHER. It's my pleasure, Corie. (*Begins to gather up wrappings and tissue paper and place them in box from coffee pot.*) It's a mother's greatest joy to be able to buy gifts for her daughter when she gets married. You'll see some day. I just hope your child doesn't deprive *you* of that pleasure.

CORIE. I'm not depriving you, Mother.

MOTHER. I didn't say you were.

CORIE. (*Moves down to* MOTHER.) Yes, you did.

MOTHER. Then why are you?

CORIE. Because I think you should spend the money on yourself, that's why.

MOTHER. Myself? What does a woman like me need? Living all alone . . . Way out in New Jersey. (*Picks up box with wrappings and places it outside front door.*)

CORIE. (*Follows* MOTHER.) It's only been six days. And you're five minutes from the city.

MOTHER. Who can get through that traffic in five minutes?

CORIE. Then why don't you move into New York?

MOTHER. Where . . . ? Where would I live?

CORIE. Mother, I don't care where you live. The point is, you've got to start living for yourself now . . . (MOTHER *moves back into room.*) Mother, the whole world has just opened up to you. Why don't you travel? You've got the time, the luggage. All you need are the shots.

MOTHER. (*Sits on suitcase.*) Travel! . . . You think it's so easy for a woman of my age to travel alone?

CORIE. You'll meet people.

MOTHER. I read a story in the Times. A middle-aged woman travelling alone fell off the deck of a ship. They never discovered it until they got to France.

CORIE. (*Moves L. and turns back to* MOTHER.) I promise you, Mother, if *you* fell off a ship, *someone* would know about it.

MOTHER. I thought I might get myself a job.

CORIE. (*Straws in the wind.*) Hey, that's a great idea. (*Sits on paint can.*)

MOTHER. (*Shrugs, defeated.*) What would I do?

CORIE. I don't know what you would do. What would you *like* to do?

MOTHER. (*Considers.*) I'd like to be a grandmother. I think that would be nice.

CORIE. A grandmother?? . . . What's your rush? You know, underneath that Army uniform, you're still a young, vital woman . . . Do you know what I think you *really* need?

MOTHER. Yes, and I don't want to hear it. (*Gets up and moves away.*)

CORIE. (*Goes to her.*) Because you're afraid to hear the truth.

MOTHER. It's not the truth I'm afraid to hear. It's the *word* you're going to use.

CORIE. You're darn right I'm going to use that word . . . It's love!

MOTHER. Oh . . . Thank you.

CORIE. A week ago I didn't know what it meant. And then I checked into the Plaza Hotel. For six wonderful days . . . And do you know what happened to me there?

MOTHER. I promised myself I wouldn't ask.

CORIE. I found *love* . . . spiritual, emotional and physical love. And I don't think anyone on earth should be without it.

MOTHER. I'm not. I have you.

CORIE. I don't mean *that* kind of love. (*Moves to ladder and leans against it.*) I'm talking about late at night in . . .

MOTHER. (*Quickly.*) I *know* what you're talking about.

CORIE. Don't you even want to discuss it?

MOTHER. Not with *you* in the room.

CORIE. Well, what are you going to do about it?

MOTHER. I'm going back to New Jersey and give myself a Toni Home Permanent. Corie, sweetheart, I appreciate your concern, but I'm very happy the way I am.

CORIE. I'll be the judge of who's happy. (*They embrace.*)

(*The door flies open and* PAUL *staggers in with the bottle of scotch. He closes the door behind him and wearily leans his head against it, utterly exhausted.*)

MOTHER. Oh, Paul, you shouldn't have run . . . Just for me. (*The DOORBELL buzzes,* AUNT HARRIET'S *special buzz.*) Ooh, and there's Harriet. I've got to go. (*Picks up purse from* L. *of suitcase.*)

CORIE. Some visit.

MOTHER. Just a sneak preview. I'll see you on Friday for the World Premiere . . . (*To* PAUL.) Goodbye, Paul . . . I'm so sorry . . . (*To* CORIE.) Goodbye, love . . . I'll see you on Friday . . . (PAUL *opens the door for her.*) Thank you . . . (*Glances out at the stairs.*) Geronimo! (*Exits.*)

(PAUL *shuts door and, breathing hard, puts bottle down at foot of the ladder. He moves* L., *turns, and glares at* CORIE.)

CORIE. What is it? . . . The stairs? (PAUL *shakes his head "no."*) The hole? (PAUL *shakes his head "no."*) The bathtub? (PAUL *shakes his head "no."*) Something new? (PAUL *nods his head "yes."*) Well, what . . . ?

PAUL. (*Leaning against* U. L. *wall.*) Guess!

CORIE. Paul, I can't guess. Tell me.

PAUL. Oh, come on, Corie. Take a wild stab at it. Try something like, "All the neighbors are crazy."

CORIE. *Are* all the neighbors crazy?

PAUL. (*A pitchman's revelation.*) I just had an interesting talk with the man down in the liquor store . . . Do you know we have some of the greatest weirdos in the country right here, in this house?

CORIE. Really? Like who? (*Puts bottle on kitchen platform.*)

PAUL. (*Gathering his strength, paces* R.) Well, like to

start with, in Apartment 1C are the Boscos . . . Mr. and Mrs. J. Bosco.

CORIE. (*Moving to ladder.*) Who are they?

PAUL. (*Paces L.*) Mr. and Mrs. J. Bosco are a lovely young couple who just happen to be of the same sex and no one knows which one that is . . . (*Moves up to L. of windows.*) In Apartment 3C live Mr. and Mrs. Gonzales.

CORIE. So?

PAUL. (*Moves R. above ladder.*) I'm not through. Mr. and Mrs. Gonzales, Mr. and Mrs. Armandariz and Mr. Calhoun . . . (*Turns back to* CORIE.) who must be the umpire. (*Moves L. to L. of ladder, very secretively.*) No one knows who lives in Apartment 4D. No one has come in or gone out in three years except every morning there are nine empty cans of tuna fish outside the door . . .

CORIE. No kidding? Who do you think lives there?

PAUL. Well, it sounds like a big cat with a can opener . . . (*Gets attaché case from corner. To* CORIE.) Now there *are* one or two normal couples in the building but at this rent, *we're* not one of them.

CORIE. Well, you've got to pay for all this color and charm.

PAUL. Well, if you figure it that way, we're getting a bargain . . . (*Starts to go up stairs, turns back.*) Oh, yes. I forgot. Mr. Velasco. Victor Velasco. He lives in Apartment 6A.

CORIE. Where's 6A? (PAUL *points straight up.*) On the roof?

PAUL. Attic . . . It's an attic. (*Crosses up onto bedroom landing.*) He also skis and climbs mountains. He's 58 years old and he's known as "The Bluebeard of 48th St."

CORIE. (*Moves to stairs.*) What does that mean?

PAUL. (*Turns back to* CORIE.) Well, it either means that he's a practicing girl attacker or else he's an old man with a blue beard. (*Moves to bedroom.*) I'll say this, Corie. It's not going to be a dull two years.

CORIE. Where are you going?

PAUL. (*Turns back at bedroom door.*) I'm going to

stand in the bedroom and work. I've got to pay for all
this color and charm. If anything comes up, like the
furniture or the heat, let me know. Just let me know.
(*Bows off into bedroom and slams door.*)

CORIE. (*After a moment of thought, begins to fold up
ladder and put it against left wall.*) Can't I come in and
watch you? . . . Hey, Paul, I'm lonesome . . . (*There's
a KNOCK at the door.*) and scared!

(*As* CORIE *puts the ladder against the wall,* VICTOR
VELASCO, *58 and not breathing very hard, opens the
door and enters. It's not that he's in such good
shape. He just doesn't think about getting tired.
There are too many other things to do in the world.
He wears no top coat. Just a sport jacket, an ascot,
and a Tyrolean hat.* CORIE *turns and is startled to
find him in the room.*)

VELASCO. I beg your pardon. (*Sweeps off his hat.*) I
hope I'm not disturbing you. I don't usually do this sort
of thing but I find myself in a rather embarrassing posi-
tion and I could use your help. (*Discreetly catches his
breath.*) My name is Velasco . . . Victor Velasco.
CORIE. (*Nervously.*) Oh, yes . . . You live in the attic.
VELASCO. Yes. That's right . . . Have we met?
CORIE. (*Very nervously.*) No! . . . No, not yet.
VELASCO. Oh. Well, you see, I want to use your bedroom.
CORIE. My bedroom?
VELASCO. Yes. You see, I can't get into my apartment
and I wanted to use your window. I'll just crawl out
along the ledge.
CORIE. Oh, did you lose your key?
VELASCO. No. I have my key. I lost my money. I'm
four months behind in the rent.
CORIE. Oh! . . . Gee, that's too bad. I mean it's right
in the middle of winter . . .
VELASCO. You'll learn, as time goes by in this middle
income prison camp, that we have a rat fink for a land-

lord . . . (*Looks about the room.*) You don't have any hot coffee, do you? I'd be glad to pay you for it.

CORIE. No. We just moved in.

VELASCO. Really? (*Looks about the barren room.*) What are you, a folk singer?

CORIE. No. A wife . . . They didn't deliver our furniture yet.

VELASCO. (*Moves towards* CORIE.) You know, of course, that you're unbearably pretty. What's your name?

CORIE. Corie . . . *Mrs.* Corie Bratter.

VELASCO. (*Takes it in stride.*) You're still unbearably pretty. I may fall in love with you by seven o'clock. (*Catching sight of the hole in the skylight.*) I see the rat fink left the hole in the skylight.

CORIE. Yes, I just noticed that. (*Crosses* R., *looking up at the hole.*) But he'll fix it, won't he?

VELASCO. I wouldn't count on it. My bathtub's been running since 1949 . . . (*Moves towards* CORIE.) Does your husband work during the day?

CORIE. Yes . . . Why . . . ?

VELASCO. It's just that I'm home during the day, and I like to find out what my odds are . . . (*Scrutinizes* CORIE.) Am I making you nervous?

CORIE. (*Moving away.*) Very nervous.

VELASCO. (*Highly pleased.*) Good. Once a month, I try to make pretty young girls nervous just to keep my ego from going out. But I'll save you a lot of anguish . . . I'm 56 years old and a thoroughly nice fellow.

CORIE. Except I heard you were 58 years old. And if you're knocking off two years, I'm nervous all over again.

VELASCO. Not only pretty but bright. (*Sits down on paint can.*) I wish I were ten years older.

CORIE. Older?

VELASCO. Yes. Dirty old men seem to get away with a lot more. I'm still at the awkward stage . . . How long are you married?

CORIE. Six days—

VELASCO. In love—?

CORIE. Very much—

VELASCO. Damn . . .

CORIE. What's wrong ?

VELASCO. Under my present state of financial duress, I was hoping to be invited down soon for a free meal. But with newlyweds I could starve to death.

CORIE. Oh! Well, we'd love to have you for dinner, as soon as we get set up.

VELASCO. (*Gets up, and stepping over suitcase, moves to* CORIE.) I hate generalizations. When?

CORIE. When . . . ? Well, Friday? Is that all right?

VELASCO. Perfect. I'll be famished. I hadn't planned on eating Thursday.

CORIE. Oh, no . . . wait! On Friday night my mo— (*Thinks it over.*) Yeah. Friday night will be fine.

VELASCO. It's a date. I'll bring the wine. You can pay me for it when I get here . . . (*Moves to stairs.*) Which reminds me. You're invited to my cocktail party tonight. Ten o'clock . . . You do drink, don't you?

CORIE. Yes, of course.

VELASCO. Good. Bring liquor. (*Crosses to* CORIE *and takes her hand.*) I'll see you tonight at ten.

CORIE. (*Shivering.*) If I don't freeze to death first.

VELASCO. Oh, you don't know about the plumbing, do you? Everything in this museum works backward. (*Crosses to raised radiator on the wall.*) For instance, there's a little knob up there that says, "Important— Turn right" . . . So you turn left. (*Tries to reach it but can't.*)

CORIE. Oh, can you give me a little boost?

VELASCO. With the greatest of physical pleasure. One, two, three . . . up . . . (*Puts his arms around her, and lifts her to radiator.*) Okay?

CORIE. (*Attempting to turn knob.*) I can't quite reach—

PAUL. (*Comes out of the bedroom with affidavit in hand and his coat up over his head. Crosses to head of the stairs.*) Hey, Corie, when are they going to get here with—? (*He stops as he sees* CORIE *in* VELASCO'S *arms.*)

(VELASCO *looks at him stunned, while* CORIE *remains motionless in the air.*)

VELASCO. (*Puts* CORIE *down.*) I thought you said he works during the day.

CORIE. Oh, Paul! This is Mr. Velasco. He was just showing me how to work the radiator.

VELASCO. (*Extending his hand.*) Victor Velasco! I'm your upstairs neighbor. I'm 58 years old and a thoroughly nice fellow.

PAUL. (*Lowers his coat, and shakes hands weakly.*) Hello . . .

CORIE. Mr. Velasco was just telling me that all the plumbing works backwards.

VELASCO. That's right. An important thing to remember is, you have to flush "up." (*He demonstrates.*) With that choice bit of information, I'll make my departure. (*Crosses up onto bedroom landing.*) Don't forget. Tonight at ten.

PAUL. (*Looks at* CORIE.) What's tonight at ten?

CORIE. (*Moves to bottom of stairs.*) Oh, thanks, but I don't think so. We're expecting our furniture any minute . . . Maybe some other time.

PAUL. What's tonight at ten?

VELASCO. I'll arrange it all for you in the morning. I'm also a brilliant decorator. (*Pats* PAUL *on shoulders.*) I insist you come.

CORIE. Well, it's really very nice of you.

VELASCO. (*Crossing to bedroom door.*) I told you. I'm a very nice person. *A ce soir.* (*Exits into bedroom.*)

PAUL. (*To* CORIE.) What's tonight at ten—? (*Suddenly realizes.*) Where's he going? (*Crosses to bedroom.*)

CORIE. (*Yelling after* VELASCO.) Don't forget Friday—

PAUL. (*To* CORIE.) What's he doing in the bedroom? . . . What about Friday? (*Goes into bedroom.*)

CORIE. (*Rushes to phone and dials.*) He's coming to dinner. (*Into phone.*) Hello, Operator?

PAUL. (*Comes out of bedroom.*) That nut went out the window. (*Looks back into bedroom.*)

CORIE. I'm calling West Orange, New Jersey.

PAUL. (*Crosses down stairs to* CORIE.) Corie, did you hear what I said? There's an old nut out on our ledge.

CORIE. (*Into phone.*) 201-765-3422.

PAUL. Who are you calling?

CORIE. My mother. On Friday night, she's going to have dinner with that old nut. (VELASCO *appears on the skylight, and carefully makes his way across. Into phone.*) Hello, Jessie . . . Will you please tell my mother to call me just as soon as she gets in!

(PAUL *turns and sees* VELASCO. VELASCO *cheerfully waves and continues on his way.*)

CURTAIN

ACT II

SCENE 1

SCENE: *Seven o'clock, Friday evening. Four days later. The apartment is no longer an empty room. It is now a home. It is almost completely furnished. The room. although a pot-pourri of various periods, styles and prices is extremely tasteful and comfortable. No ultra-modern, clinical interior for* CORIE. *Each piece was selected with loving care. Since* CORIE'S *greatest aim in life is to spend as much time as possible alone with* PAUL, *she has designed the room to suit this purpose. A wrought-iron sofa stands in the middle of the room, upholstered in a bright striped fabric. It is flanked by two old-fashioned, unmatched armchairs, one with a romantically carved wooden back; the other, a bentwood chair with a black leather seat. A low, dark, wooden coffee table with carved legs is in front of the sofa, and to the Right is a small, round bentwood end table, covered in a green felt. Under the windows, a light-wood, Spanish-looking table serves as a desk, and in front of it is a bamboo, straight-back chair. A large, woven-wicker basket functions as the waste-basket. A dark, side table with lyre-shaped legs fills the wall under the radiator and below the bedroom landing, an open, cane-side table serves as a bar and telephone stand. To the Right of the windows stands a breakfront with shelves above and drawers below. The kitchen area is now partially hidden by a four-fold bamboo screen that has been backed by fabric, and potted plants have been placed in front of the screen. Straight backed bentwood chairs stand Down Right and Left. The closet has been covered by a drapery, the small windows by cafe curtains, and the skylight by a large, striped Austrian curtain. Books*

*now fill the bookcase Left of the kitchen, pictures
and decorations have been tastefully arranged on the
walls and lamps placed about the room. The bedroom landing has now been graced with a bentwood
washstand complete with pitcher and basin now filled
with a plant. In the bathroom a shower curtain and
towels have been hung, and the bedroom now boasts
a bed.*

AT RISE: *There is no one on Stage. The apartment is
dark except for a crack of LIGHT under the bedroom door, and faint MOONLIGHT from the skylight. Suddenly the front door opens and* CORIE
*rushes in, carrying a pastry box and a bag containing
two bottles. After switching on the LIGHTS at the
door, she places her packages down on the coffee
table and hangs her coat in the closet.* CORIE *now
wears a cocktail dress for the festivities planned for
tonight and she sings as she hurries to get everything ready. She is breathing heavily but she is
getting accustomed to the stairs. As she takes a bottle
of vermouth and a bottle of gin out of the bag, the
DOORBELL buzzes. She buzzes back, opens door
and yells down the stairs.*

CORIE. (*Yells.*) Paul? (*We hear some strange, inco-
herent sound from below.*) Hi, love. . . . (*Crosses back
to coffee table, and dumps hors d'oeuvres from pastry box
onto tray.*) Hey, they sent the wrong lamps . . . but
they go with the room so I'm keeping them. (*Crosses to
bar, gets martini pitcher and brings it back to coffee
table.*) Oh, do you have an Aunt Fern? . . . Because she
sent us a check . . . Anyway, you have a cheap Aunt
Fern . . . How you doing? (*We hear MUMBLE from
below. She opens both bottles and pours them simultane-
ously into the shaker so that she now has cocktails made
with equal parts.*) Oh, and your mother called from Philly
. . . She and Dad will be up a week from Sunday . . .
And your sister has a new boy friend. From Rutgers . . .

He's got acne and they all hate him . . . including your sister. (*Takes the shaker and, mixing the cocktails, she crosses to the door.*) Hey, lover, start puckering your lips 'cause you're gonna get kissed for five solid minutes and then . . . (*Stops.*) Oh, hello, Mr. Munshin. I thought it was my husband. Sorry. (*A door slams. She shrugs sheepishly and walks back into the room, closing the door behind her. As she goes up into the kitchen, the door opens and* PAUL *enters, gasping. He drops his attaché case at the railing, and collapses on the couch.* CORIE *comes out of kitchen with shaker and ice bucket.*) It *was* you. I thought I heard your voice. (*Puts ice bucket on bookcase and shaker on end table.*)

PAUL. (*Gasp, gasp.*) Mr. Munshin and I came in together. (CORIE *jumps on him and flings her arms around his neck. He winces in pain.*) Do you have to carry on—a whole personal conversation with me—on the stairs?

CORIE. Well, there's so much I wanted to tell you . . . and I haven't seen you all day . . . and it takes you so long to get up.

PAUL. Everyone knows the intimate details of our life . . . I ring the bell and suddenly we're on the air.

CORIE. Tomorrow I'll yell, "Come on up, Harry, my husband isn't home." (*Takes empty box and bag and throws them in garbage pail in kitchen.*) Hey, wouldn't that be a gas if everyone in the building thought I was having an affair with someone?

PAUL. Mr. Munshin thinks it's *him* right now.

CORIE. (*Crossing back to couch.*) Well?

PAUL. Well what?

CORIE. What happened in court today? Gump or Birnbaum?

PAUL. Birnbaum!

CORIE. (*Jumps on his lap again. He winces again.*) Oh, Paul, you won. You won, darling. Oh, sweetheart, I'm so proud of you. (*Stops and looks at him.*) Well, aren't you happy?

PAUL. (*Glumly.*) Birnbaum won the protection of his good name but no damages. We were awarded six cents.

CORIE. Six cents?

PAUL. That's the law. You have to be awarded something so the court made it six cents.

CORIE. How much of that do you get?

PAUL. Nothing. Birnbaum gets the whole six cents . . . And I get a going over in the office. From now on I get all the cases that come in for a dime or under.

CORIE. (*Opening his collar and rubbing his neck.*) Oh, darling, you won. That's all that counts. You're a good lawyer.

PAUL. Some lawyer . . . So tomorrow I go back to sharpening pencils.

CORIE. And tonight you're here with me. (*Kisses his neck.*) Did you miss me today?

PAUL. No.

CORIE. (*Gets off his lap and sits on couch.*) Why not?

PAUL. Because you called me eight times . . . I don't speak to you that much when I'm home.

CORIE. (*Rearranging canapes.*) Oh, you're grouchy. I want a divorce.

PAUL. I'm not grouchy . . . I'm tired . . . I had a rotten day today . . . I'm a little irritable . . . and cold . . . and grouchy.

CORIE. Okay, grouch. I'll fix you a drink. (*Crosses to bar and brings back three glasses.*)

PAUL. (*Crosses to closet and takes off overcoat and jacket and hangs them up.*) I just couldn't think today. Couldn't think . . . Moving furniture until three o'clock in the morning.

CORIE. Mr. Velasco moved. You complained. (*Pours drink.*)

PAUL. Mr. Velasco *pointed! I* moved! . . . He came in here, drank my liquor, made three telephone calls, and ordered me around like I was one of the Santini Brothers. (*Takes drink from* CORIE, *and crosses to dictionary on table under the radiator. Takes gulp of drink and reacts with horror. Looks at* CORIE, *and she shrugs in reply.*)

CORIE. Temper, temper. We're supposed to be charming tonight.

PAUL. (*Taking tie off.*) Yeah, well, I've got news for you. This thing tonight has fiasco written all over it.

CORIE. (*Moves to mirror on washstand on bedroom landing.*) Why should it be a fiasco? It's just conceivable they may have something in common.

PAUL. (*Folding tie.*) Your mother? That quiet, dainty little woman . . . and the Count of Monte Cristo? You must be kidding. (*Puts tie between pages of dictionary. Slams dictionary.*)

CORIE. Why? (*Puts on necklace and earrings.*)

PAUL. (*Crosses to closet and gets another tie.*) You saw his apartment. He wears Japanese kimonos and sleeps on rugs. Your mother wears a hair net and sleeps on a board.

CORIE. What's that got to do with it?

PAUL. (*Crossing back to mirror under radiator and fixing tie.*) Everything. He skis, climbs mountains, and the only way in to his apartment is up a ladder or across a ledge. I don't really think he's looking for a good cook with a bad back.

CORIE. The possibility of anything permanent never even occurred to me.

PAUL. Permanent? We're lucky if we get past seven o'clock— (*The doorbell BUZZES and* PAUL *crosses to door.*)

CORIE. That's her. Now you've got me worried . . . Paul, did I do something horrible?

PAUL. (*Buzzing downstairs.*) Probably.

CORIE. Well, do something. Don't answer the door. Maybe she'll go home.

PAUL. Too late. I buzzed. I could put a few nembutals in his drink. It won't stop him but it could slow him down. (*Opens door and yells downstairs.*) Mom?

MOTHER'S VOICE. (*From far below.*) Yes, dear . . .

PAUL. (*Yelling through hands.*) Take your time. (*Turns back into room.*) She's at Camp Three. She'll try the final assault in a few minutes.

CORIE. Paul, maybe we could help her. (*Coming down stairs.*)

PAUL. (*Getting blazer out of closet.*) What do you mean?

CORIE. (*Above couch.*) A woman puts on rouge and powder to make her face more attractive. Maybe we can put some make-up on her personality.

PAUL. (*Puts attaché case aside on bookcase.*) I don't think I want to hear the rest of this.

CORIE. All I'm saying is, we don't have to come right out and introduce her as "my dull 50-year-old housewife mother."

PAUL. (*Crosses to bar and pours a drink of scotch.*) Well, that wasn't the wording I had planned. What did you have in mind?

CORIE. (*Moves around couch and sits* R. *of couch.*) Something a little more glamorous . . . A former actress.

PAUL. Corie—

CORIE. Well, she *was* in "The Man Who Came To Dinner."

PAUL. Your mother? In "The Man Who Came To Dinner"? . . . Where, in the West Orange P.T.A. show? (*Moves to couch.*)

CORIE. No! . . . On Broadway . . . And she was in the original company of "Strange Interlude" and she had a small singing part in "Knickerbocker Holiday."

PAUL. Are you serious?

CORIE. Honestly. Cross my heart.

PAUL. Your mother? An actress? (*Sits next to* CORIE.) CORIE. Yes.

PAUL. Why didn't you ever tell me?

CORIE. I didn't think you'd be interested.

PAUL. That's fascinating. I can't get over it.

CORIE. You see. *Now* you're interested in her.

PAUL. It's a lie?

CORIE. The whole thing.

PAUL. I'm going to control myself. (*Gets up and crosses up above the couch.*)

CORIE. (*Up and crosses to him* R. *of couch.*) What do you say? Is she an actress?

PAUL. No. (*Moves towards door.*)

CORIE. A fashion designer. The brains behind Ann Fogarty.

PAUL. (*Points to door.*) She's on her way up.

CORIE. A mystery writer . . . under an assumed name.

PAUL. Let's lend her my trench coat and say she's a private eye.

CORIE. You're no help.

PAUL. I didn't book this act.

CORIE. (*Moves to* PAUL.) Paul, who is she going to be?

PAUL. She's going to be your mother . . . and the evening will eventually pass . . . It just means . . . that the Birdman of 48th Street is not going to be your father. (*Opens door.*) Hello, Mom.

(*The* MOTHER *collapses in and* PAUL *and* CORIE *rush to support her.* PAUL *and* CORIE *quickly lead* MOTHER *to armchair* R. *of couch.*)

CORIE. Hello, sweetheart, how are you? (*Kisses* MOTHER, *who gasps for air.*) Are you all right? (MOTHER *nods.*) You want some water?

(MOTHER *shakes head, "No," as* PAUL *and* CORIE *lower her into chair. She drops pocketbook on floor.*)

MOTHER. Paul . . . in my pocketbook . . . are some pink pills.

PAUL. (*Picks up bag, closes door and begins to look for pills.*) Pink pills . . .

(CORIE *helps* MOTHER *off with her coat.*)

MOTHER. I'll be all right . . . Just a little out of breath . . . (CORIE *crosses to coffee table and pours a drink.*) I had to park the car six blocks away . . . then it started to rain so I ran the last two blocks . . . then my heel got caught in the subway grating . . . so I pulled my foot out and stepped in a puddle . . . then a cab went by and splashed my stockings . . . if the hardware store downstairs was open . . . I was going to buy a knife and kill myself.

(PAUL *gives her the pill, and* CORIE *gives her the drink.*)

CORIE. Here, Mom. Drink this down.

PAUL. Here's the pill . . . (MOTHER *takes pill, drinks and coughs.*)

MOTHER. A martini? To wash down a pill?

CORIE. It'll make you feel better.

MOTHER. I *had* a martini at home. It made me sick . . . That's why I'm taking the pill . . .

(CORIE *puts drink down on table.*)

PAUL. (*Sitting on end table.*) You must be exhausted.

MOTHER. I'd just like to crawl into bed and cry myself to sleep.

CORIE. (*Offering her tray of hors d'oeuvre.*) Here, Mom, have an hors d'oeuvre.

MOTHER. No, thank you, dear.

CORIE. It's just blue cheese and sour cream.

MOTHER. (*Holds stomach.*) I wish you hadn't said that.

PAUL. She doesn't feel like it, Corie . . . (CORIE *puts tray down and sits on couch. To* MOTHER.) Maybe you'd like to lie down?

CORIE. (*Panicky.*) Now? She can't lie down now.

MOTHER. Corie's right. I can't lie down without my board . . . (*Puts gloves into pocket of coat.*) Right now all I want to do is see the apartment.

PAUL. (*Sitting on couch.*) That's right. You haven't seen it with its clothes on, have you?

MOTHER. (*Rises and moves* L.) Oh, Corie . . . Corie . . .

CORIE. She doesn't like it.

MOTHER. (*Exhausted sinks into armchair* L. *of couch.*) Like it? It's magnificent . . . and in less than a week. My goodness, how did you manage? Where did you get your ideas from?

PAUL. We have a decorator who comes in through the window once a week.

CORIE. (*Crossing up to bedroom.*) Come take a look at the bedroom.

MOTHER. (*Crossing up to bedroom.*) Yes, that's what I want to do . . . look at the bedroom. Were you able to get the bed in? (*Looks into room.*) Oh, it just fits, doesn't it?

PAUL. (*Moves to stairs.*) Just. We have to turn in unison.

MOTHER. It looks very snug . . . And did you find a way to get to the closet?

CORIE. Oh, we decided not to use the closet for a while.

MOTHER. Really? Don't you need the space?

PAUL. Not as much as we need the clothes. It's flooded.

MOTHER. The closet flooded?

CORIE. It was an accident. Mr. Velasco left his bathtub running.

MOTHER. (*Moving down stairs.*) Mr. Velasco? . . . Oh, the man upstairs—

PAUL. (*Taking her arm.*) Oh, then you know about Mr. Velasco?

MOTHER. Oh, yes. Corie had me on the phone for two hours.

PAUL. Did you know he's been married three times?

MOTHER. Yes . . . (*Turns back to* CORIE.) If I were you, dear, I'd sleep with a gun. (*Sits in bentwood armchair.*)

PAUL. Well, there's just one thing I want to say about this evening . . .

CORIE. (*Quickly as she crosses to coffee table.*) Er . . . not before you have a drink. (*Hands* MOTHER *martini.*) Come on, Mother. To toast our new home.

MOTHER. (*Holding glass.*) Well, I can't refuse that.

CORIE. (*Making toast.*) To the wonderful new life that's ahead of us all.

PAUL. (*Holds up his glass.*) And to the best sport I've ever seen. Your mother.

MOTHER. (*Making toast.*) And to two very charming people . . . that I'm so glad to be seeing again tonight . . . your mother and father.

(CORIE *sinks down on sofa.*)

PAUL. (*About to drink, stops.*) My what?

MOTHER. Your mother and father.

PAUL. What about my mother and father?

MOTHER. Well, we're having dinner with them tonight. aren't we . . . ? (*To* CORIE.) Corie, isn't that what you said?

PAUL. (*Sits next to* CORIE *on sofa.*) Is that right, Corie? Is that what you said?

CORIE. (*Looks helpless, then plunges in.*) Well, if I told you it was a blind date with Mr. Velasco upstairs, I couldn't have blasted you out of the house.

MOTHER. A blind date . . . (*Doesn't quite get it yet.*) With Mr. Velasco . . . (*Then the dawn.*) The one that . . . ? (*She points up, then panics.*) Good God! (*Takes a big gulp of her martini.*)

PAUL. (*To* CORIE.) You didn't even tell your mother?

CORIE. I was going to tell her the truth.

PAUL. (*Looks at watch.*) It's one minute to seven. That's cutting it pretty thin, isn't it?

MOTHER. Corie, how could you do this to me? Of all the people in the world . . .

CORIE. (*Gets up and moves to* MOTHER.) I don't see what you're making such a fuss about. He's just a man.

MOTHER. My *accountant's* just a man. You make him sound like Douglas Fairbanks, Junior.

CORIE. He looks *nothing* like Douglas Fairbanks, Junior . . . does he, Paul?

PAUL. No . . . He just jumps like him.

MOTHER. I'm not even dressed.

CORIE. (*Brushing* MOTHER's *clothes.*) You look fine, Mother.

MOTHER. For Paul's parents I just wanted to look clean . . . *He'll* think I'm a nurse.

CORIE. Look, Mother, I promise you you'll have a good time tonight. He's a sweet, charming and intelligent man. If you'll just relax I *know* you'll have a perfectly nice evening. (*There is a KNOCK on the door.*) Besides, it's too late. He's here.

MOTHER. Oh, no—

CORIE. All right, now don't get excited.

MOTHER. (*Gets up and puts drink on coffee table.*) You could say I'm the cleaning woman . . . I'll dust the table. Give me five dollars and I'll leave. (*Starts up stairs to bedroom.*)

CORIE. (*Stops her on stairs.*) You just stay here—

PAUL. (*Going to* MOTHER.) It's going to be fine, Mom. (*Crosses to door.*)

CORIE. (*Leads* MOTHER *back to sofa.*) And smile. You're irresistible when you do. And finish your martini. (*Takes it from table and hands it to* MOTHER.)

MOTHER. Do you have a lot of these?

CORIE. As many as you need.

MOTHER. I'm going to need a lot of these. (*Downs a good belt.*)

PAUL. Can I open the door?

CORIE. Paul, wait a minute . . . Mother . . . your hair . . . in the back . . .

MOTHER. (*Stricken, begins to fuss with hair.*) What? What's the matter with my hair?

CORIE. (*Fixing* MOTHER's *hair.*) It's all right now. I fixed it.

MOTHER. (*Moves towards* PAUL.) Is something wrong with my hair?

PAUL. (*Impatient.*) There's a man standing out there.

CORIE. Wait a minute, Paul . . . (PAUL *moves back into room and leans against back of armchair. Turns* MOTHER *to her.*) Now, Mother . . . The only thing I'd like to suggest is . . . well . . . just try and go along with everything.

MOTHER. What do you mean? Where are we going?

CORIE. I don't know. But wherever it is . . . just relax . . . and be one of the fellows.

MOTHER. One of what fellows?

CORIE. I mean, don't worry about your stomach.

(*There is another KNOCK on the door.*)

MOTHER. Oh, my stomach. (*Sinks down on couch.*)

PAUL. Can I open the door now?

CORIE. (*Moving to* R. *of the couch.*) Okay, okay . . . open the door.

(PAUL *nods gratefully, then opens the door.* VELASCO *stands there looking quite natty in a double-breasted, blue, pin-striped suit. He carries a small, covered frying pan in a gloved hand.*)

PAUL. Oh, sorry to keep you waiting, Mr. Velasco. Come on in—

VELASCO. (*Moving into well, to* PAUL.) Ah! *Ho si mah ling* . . .

PAUL. No, no . . . It's Paul.

VELASCO. I know. I was just saying hello in Chinese . . .

PAUL. Oh . . . hello.

VELASCO. (*To* CORIE.) Corie, rava-shing . . .

CORIE. (*Enthralled.*) Oh . . . What does that mean?

VELASCO. Ravishing. That's English.

CORIE. (*Taken aback.*) Oh . . . Ah, Paul . . . Would you do the honors?

PAUL. Yes, of course. Mr. Velasco, I'd like you to meet Corie's mother, Mrs. Banks . . . (CORIE *steps back unveiling* MOTHER *with a gesture.*) Mother, this is our new neighbor, Mr. Velasco . . .

MOTHER. How do you do?

VELASCO. (*Sweeps to* MOTHER, *takes her hand and bows ever so slightly.*) Mrs. Banks . . . I've been looking forward so to meeting you. I invite your daughter to my cocktail party and she spends the entire evening talking of nothing but you.

(CORIE *moves* U. L. *of couch taking it all in with great pleasure.*)

MOTHER. Oh . . . ? It must have been a dull party.

VELASCO. Not in the least.

MOTHER. I mean if she did nothing but talk about me . . . *That* must have been dull. Not the party.

(PAUL *moves above couch to coffee table and gets his drink.*)

VELASCO. I understand.

MOTHER. Thank you . . .

CORIE. (*To the rescue.*) Oh, is that for us?

VELASCO. Yes . . . I couldn't get the wine . . . my credit stopped . . . so instead . . . (*Puts pan down on end table and with a flourish lifts cover.*) Knichi!

MOTHER. Knichi?

CORIE. It's an hors d'oeuvre. Mr. Velasco makes them himself. He's a famous gourmet.

MOTHER. A gourmet . . . Imagine!

VELASCO. This won second prize last year at the Venice Food Festival.

MOTHER. Second prize . . .

CORIE. Mr. Velasco once cooked for the King of Sweden, Mother.

MOTHER. Really? Did you work for him?

VELASCO. No . . . We belong to the same club.

MOTHER. (*Embarrassed.*) The same club . . . Of course.

VELASCO. It's a Gourmet Society. There's a hundred and fifty of us.

MOTHER. All gourmets . . .

VELASCO. That includes the King, Prince Philip and Darryl Zanuck.

MOTHER. Darryl Zanuck too.

VELASCO. We meet once every five years for a dinner that we cook ourselves. In 1987 they're supposed to come to my house. (*Looks at his watch.*) We have another thirty seconds . . .

PAUL. Until what?

VELASCO. Until they're edible. (*Takes cover off pan, and puts it on end table.*) Now . . . the last fifteen seconds we just let them sit there and breathe . . .

CORIE. (*Moves* R.) Gee, they look marvelous.

VELASCO. When you eat this, you take a bite into history. Knichi is over two thousand years old . . . Not this particular batch, of course.

(*He laughs, but* MOTHER *laughs too loud and too long.*)

CORIE. (*Again to the rescue.*) Wow, what a great smell . . . (*To* VELASCO.) Mr. Velasco, would you be a traitor to the Society if you told us what's in it?

VELASCO. (*Secretively.*) Well, if caught, it's punishable by a cold salad at the dinner . . . but since I'm among friends, it's bits of salted fish, grated olives, spices and onion biscuits . . . (MOTHER *reacts unhappily to the list of ingredients. Looks at watch once more.*) Ah, ready . . . Five, four, three, two, one . . . (*Holds pan out to* MOTHER.) Mrs. Banks?

MOTHER. (*Tentatively.*) Oh . . . thank you. (*She takes one and raises it slowly to her mouth.*)

CORIE. What kind of fish?

VELASCO. Eel!

PAUL. Eel?

MOTHER. (*Crumples with distaste.*) Eel?? (*She doesn't eat it.*)

VELASCO. That's why the time element is so essential. Eel spoils quickly. (MOTHER *crumples even more.*) Mrs. Banks, you're not eating.

MOTHER. My throat's a little dry. Maybe if I finish my martini first . . .

VELASCO. No, no . . . That will never do. The temperature of the knichi is very important. It must be now. In five minutes we throw it away.

MOTHER. Oh! . . . Well, I wouldn't want you to do that. (*Looks at the knichi, then starts to take a nibble.*)

VELASCO. Pop it!

MOTHER. I beg your pardon.

VELASCO. (*Puts down pan and takes off cooking glove.*) If you nibble at knichi, it tastes bitter. You must pop it. (*He takes a knichi and tosses it from hand to hand three or four times and then pops it into his mouth.*) You see.

MOTHER. Oh, yes.

(*She tosses knichi from hand to hand a few times and then tries to pop it into her mouth. But she misses and it flies over her shoulder. VELASCO quickly offers her another. Although this time she succeeds in getting it into her mouth, she chokes on it.*)

CORIE. (*Sitting next to her.*) Mother, are you all right?

MOTHER. (*Coughing.*) I think I popped it back too far.

CORIE. (*Takes drink from PAUL and hands it to MOTHER.*) Here . . . Drink this.

MOTHER. (*Drinks, gasps.*) Ooh . . . Was that my martini?

PAUL. (*Gets up and retrieves drink.*) No. My scotch.

MOTHER. Oh, my stomach.

VELASCO. (*Moving L. above couch.*) The trick is to pop it right to the center of the tongue . . . Then it gets the benefit of the entire palate . . . Corie? (*Offers her the dish.*)

CORIE. (*Takes one.*) Well, here goes. (*Tosses it back and forth, then pops it perfectly.*) How about that?

VELASCO. Perfect. You're the prettiest epicurean I've ever seen . . . (*Offers knichi to PAUL.*) Paul?

PAUL. Er, no thank you. I have a bad arm.

CORIE. You can *try* it. You should try everything, right, Mr. Velasco?

VELASCO. As the French say, "At least once" . . . (*PAUL pulls up his sleeve, takes a knichi . . . then bites into it.*) Agh . . . Bitter, right?

CORIE. You know why, don't you?

PAUL. I didn't pop! I nibbled!

CORIE. Try another one and pop it.

PAUL. I don't want to pop another one. Besides, I think we're over the five-minute limit now anyway.

VELASCO. (*Crossing to MOTHER behind couch, leans over to her very confidentially.*) Taste is something that must be cultivated.

MOTHER. (*Almost jumps.*) Er, yes, I've often said that . . .

CORIE. Well, are we ready to go out to dinner?

MOTHER. (*Nervously.*) You mean we're going out?

CORIE. We had a fire in our stove.

MOTHER. What happened?

PAUL. Nothing. We just turned it on.

CORIE. Mother, are you hungry?

MOTHER. Not terribly . . . no.

CORIE. Paul, you're the host. Suggest someplace.

PAUL. Well . . . er . . . how about Marty's on 47th St.?

CORIE. Marty's? That barn? You get a cow and a baked potato. What kind of a suggestion was that?

PAUL. I'm sorry. I didn't know it was a trick question.

CORIE. Tonight has to be something special. Mr. Velasco, you must know someplace different and unusual . . .

VELASCO. (*Leaning against end table.*) Unusual? Yes, I know a very unusual place. It's the best food in New York. But I'm somewhat hesitant to suggest . . .

CORIE. Oh, please. (*To* MOTHER.) What do you say, Mother? Do you feel adventurous?

MOTHER. You know me, one of the fellows.

CORIE. (*To* VELASCO.) There you are. We place the evening in your hands.

VELASCO. A delightful proposition . . . For dinner, we go to the Four Winds.

PAUL. Oh! The Chinese Restaurant? On Fifty-third Street?

VELASCO. No . . . The Albanian restaurant on Staten Island.

MOTHER. (*Holds stomach.*) Staten Island?

CORIE. Doesn't it sound wild, Mother?

MOTHER. Yes . . . wild.

CORIE. I love it already. (*As she sweeps past* PAUL, *on her way to bedroom, she punches him on the shoulder.*)

VELASCO. (*Sitting next to* MOTHER.) Don't expect anything lavish in the way of decor. But Uzu will take care of the atmosphere.

MOTHER. Who's Uzu?

VELASCO. It's a Greek liquor . . . Deceptively powerful. I'll only allow you one.

MOTHER. Oh . . . thank you.

CORIE. (*Coming out of bedroom with coat and purse.*) It sounds perfect . . . Let's go.

PAUL. It'll be murder getting a cab now.

VELASCO. I'll worry about the transportation. All you have to do is pick up the check.

CORIE. (*Above couch.*) Mother has her car.

VELASCO. (*Rises, to* PAUL.) You see? My job is done. Mrs. Banks . . . (*Holds up her coat.*)

(PAUL *crosses to closet and gets overcoat.*)

MOTHER. (*Putting on coat.*) Mr. Velasco, don't you wear a coat?

VELASCO. Only in the winter.

MOTHER. It's thirty-five.

VELASCO. (*Taking beret out of pocket.*) For 25 I wear a coat . . . For 35 . . . (*Puts beret on. Crosses to door taking scarf out of pocket with a great flair.* PAUL *watches with great distaste and then crosses into bedroom. Opens door.*) Ready? . . . My group stay close to me. If anyone gets lost, we'll meet at the United States Embassy. (*Flings scarf about his neck and exits.*)

(MOTHER *desperately clutches* CORIE's *arm, but* CORIE *manages to push her out the door.*)

CORIE. (*Turning back for* PAUL.) What are you looking for?

PAUL. (*Comes out of bedroom.*) My gloves . . .

CORIE. (*With disdain.*) You don't need gloves. It's only thirty-five. (*She sweeps out.*)

PAUL. That's right. I forgot. (*Mimicking* VELASCO, *he flings his scarf around his neck as he crosses to the door.*) We're having a heat wave. (*He turns off the LIGHTS and slams the door shut.*)

CURTAIN

(In the dark we hear the splash of WAVES and the melancholy toots of FOG HORNS in the harbor sounding almost as sad as PAUL *and the* MOTHER *must be feeling at this moment.)*

ACT II

SCENE 2

SCENE: *About 2 P.M. The apartment is still dark.*
AT RISE: *We hear LAUGHTER on the stairs. The door opens and* CORIE *rushes in. She is breathless, hysterical, and wearing* VELASCO'S *beret and scarf.*

CORIE. Whoo . . . I beat you . . . I won. (*She turns on the LIGHTS, crosses to the couch and collapses.*)

(VELASCO *rushes in after her, breathless and laughing.*)

VELASCO. (*Sinking to floor in front of couch.*) It wasn't a fair race. You tickled me.
CORIE. Ooh . . . Ooh, I feel good. Except my tongue keeps rolling up. And when I talk it rolls back out like a noisemaker.
VELASCO. That's a good sign. It shows the food was seasoned properly.
CORIE. Hey, tell me how to say it again.
VELASCO. Say what?
CORIE. "Waiter, there's a fly in my soup."
VELASCO. Oh. *"Poopla . . . sirca al mercoori."*
CORIE. That's right. *"Sirca . . . poopla al mercoori."*
VELASCO. No, no. That's "Fly, I have a waiter in my soup."
CORIE. Well, I did. He put in his hand to take out the fly. (*Rises to her knees.*) Boy, I like that singer . . . *Sways back and forth as she sings.*) "Shama . . . shama . . ela mai kemama" . . . (*Flings her coat onto couch.* VELASCO *rises to a sitting position, crosses his legs and*

plays an imaginary flute.) Hey, what am I singing, anyway?

VELASCO. (*Stretches prone on the floor.*) It's an old Albanian folk song.

CORIE. (*Impressed with her own virtuosity.*) "*Shama shama . . ."?* No kidding? What does it mean?

VELASCO. "Jimmy cracked corn and I don't care."

CORIE. Well, I don't. (*Feels her head.*) Oh, boy . . . How many ZuZus did I have? Three or four?

VELASCO. *Uzus!* . . . Nine or ten.

CORIE. Then it was ten 'cause I thought I had four . . . How is my head going to feel in the morning?

VELASCO. Wonderful.

CORIE. No headaches?

VELASCO. No headache . . . But you won't be able to make a fist for three days. (*He raises his hand and demonstrates by not being able to make a fist.*)

CORIE. (*Holds out both hands and looks at them.*) Yeah. Look at that. Stiff as a board. (*Climbs off couch, onto floor next to* VELASCO.) What do they put in Uzu anyway?

VELASCO. (*Holding up stiff hands.*) I think it's starch.

CORIE. (*Looks at her two stiff hands.*) Hey, how about a game of ping pong? We can play doubles. (CORIE *swings her two stiff hands at an imaginary ball.*)

VELASCO. Not now. (*Sits up.*) We're supposed to do something important. What was it?

CORIE. What was it? (*Ponders, then remembers.*) Oh! . . . We're supposed to make coffee. (CORIE *places the shoes she has taken off under the sofa and moves towards the kitchen.*)

VELASCO. (*Following her.*) I'll make it. What kind do you have?

CORIE. Instant Maxwell House.

VELASCO. (*Crushed.*) *Instant* coffee?

(*He holds his brow with his stiff hands. He and* CORIE *disappear behind the screened kitchen continuing their babbling. Suddenly we hear scuffling in the hall-*

way and PAUL *struggles in through the door carrying the* MOTHER *in his arms. From* PAUL'S *staggering we'd guess that the* MOTHER *must now weigh about two thousand pounds. He makes it to the sofa, where he drops her, and then in utter exhaustion sinks to the floor below her. They* BOTH *stare unseeing, and suck desperately for air.* CORIE *and* VELASCO *emerge from the kitchen with* VELASCO *carrying a coffee pot.*)

CORIE. (*Crosses to* MOTHER.) Forgot the stove doesn't work. Upstairs everyone . . . for coffee. (CORIE *pulls* MOTHER'S *coat but there is no reaction from* MOTHER *or* PAUL.) Don't you want coffee?

(PAUL *and* MOTHER *shake their heads, "No."*)

VELASCO. (*Going to door.*) They'll drink it if we make it . . .

CORIE. (*Following him.*) Don't you two go away . . .

(CORIE *and* VELASCO *exit with* BOTH *joining in "Shama, Shama."* PAUL *and* MOTHER *stare silently ahead. They appear to be in shock, having gone through some terrible ordeal.*)

MOTHER. (Finally.) I feel like we've died . . . and gone to heaven . . . only we had to climb up . . .

PAUL. (*Gathering his strength.*) Struck down in the prime of life . . .

MOTHER. I don't really feel sick . . . Just kind of numb . . . and I can't make a fist . . . (*She holds up a stiff hand.*)

PAUL. You want to hear something frightening? . . . My teeth feel soft . . . It's funny . . . but the best thing we had all night was the knichi.

MOTHER. Anyway, Corie had a good time . . . Don't you think Corie had a good time, Paul?

PAUL. (*Struggling up onto couch* L. *of* MOTHER.) Wonderful . . . Poor kid . . . It isn't often we get out to Staten Island in February.

MOTHER. She seems to get such a terrific kick out of living. You've got to admire that, don't you, Paul?

PAUL. I admire anyone who has three portions of poofla-poo pie.

MOTHER. (*Starts.*) What's poofla-poo pie?

PAUL. Don't you remember? That gook that came in a turban.

MOTHER. I thought that was the waiter . . . I tried, Paul. But I just couldn't seem to work up an appetite the way they did.

PAUL. (*Reassuring her.*) No, no, Mom . . . You mustn't blame yourself . . . We're just not used to that kind of food . . . You just don't pick up your fork and dig into a *brown* salad . . . You've got to play around with it for a while.

MOTHER. Maybe I *am* getting old . . . I don't mind telling you it's very discouraging . . . (*With great difficulty, she manages to rouse herself and get up from the couch.*) Anyway, I don't think I could get through coffee . . . I'm all out of pink pills . . .

PAUL. Where are you going?

MOTHER. Home . . . I want to die in my own bed. (*Exhausted, she sinks into chair.*)

PAUL. Well, what'll I tell them?

MOTHER. Oh, make up some clever little lie. (*Rallies herself, gets up.*) Tell Corie I'm not really her mother. She'll probably never want to see me again anyway . . . Good night, dear. (*Just as* MOTHER *gets to the door, it opens and* CORIE *and* VELASCO *return.*) Oh, coffee ready? (*She turns back into the room.* VELASCO *crosses to the bar, as* CORIE *moves above the couch.*)

CORIE. I was whistling the Armenian National Anthem and I blew out the pilot light.

VELASCO. (*Puts four brandy snifters he has brought in down on bar and, taking decanter from bar, begins to pour brandy.*) Instead we're going to have flaming brandy . . . Corie, give everyone a match.

(CORIE *moves to side table.*)

MOTHER. I'm afraid you'll have to excuse me, dear. It *is* a little late.

CORIE. (*Moves towards* MOTHER.) Mother, you're not going home. It's the shank of the evening.

MOTHER. I know, but I've got a ten o'clock dentist appointment . . . at nine o'clock . . . and it's been a very long evening . . . What I mean is it's late, but I've had a wonderful time . . . I don't know what I'm saying.

CORIE. But, Mother—

MOTHER. Darling, I'll call you in the morning. Good night, Paul . . . Good night, Mr. Velasco . . .

VELASCO. (*Putting down brandy, crosses to* CORIE.) Good night, Paul . . . Good night, Corie . . .

CORIE. Mr. Velasco, you're not going too?

VELASCO. (*Taking beret and scarf from* CORIE *and putting them on.*) Of course. I'm driving Mrs. Banks home.

MOTHER. (*Moves away in shock.*) *Oh, no!* (*Recovers herself and turns back.*) I mean, oh, no, it's too late.

VELASCO. (*To* MOTHER.) Too late for what?

MOTHER. The buses. They stop running at two. How will you get home?

VELASCO. Why worry about it now? I'll meet that problem in New Jersey.

(VELASCO *moves to the door and* CORIE *in great jubilation flings herself over the back of the couch.*)

MOTHER. But it's such a long trip . . . (*Crosses to* CORIE.) Corie, isn't it a long trip?

CORIE. Not really. It's only about thirty minutes.

MOTHER. But it's such an inconvenience. Really, Mr. Velasco, it's very sweet of you but—

VELASCO. Victor!

MOTHER. What?

VELASCO. If we're going to spend the rest of the evening together, it must be Victor.

MOTHER. Oh!

VELASCO. And I insist the arrangement be reciprocal. What is it?

MOTHER. What is what?

CORIE. Your name, Mother. (*To* VELASCO.) It's Ethel.

MOTHER. Oh, that's right. Ethel. My name is Ethel.

VELASCO. That's better . . . Now . . . are we ready
. . . Ethel?

MOTHER. Well . . . if you insist, Walter.

VELASCO. Victor! It's Victor.

MOTHER. Yes. Victor!

VELASCO. Good night, Paul . . . *Shama shama,* Corie.

CORIE. *Shama shama!*

VELASCO. (*Moves to door.*) If you don't hear from us
in a week, we'll be at the Nacional Hotel in Mexico City
. . . Room 703! . . . Let's go, Ethel! (*And he goes out
the door. The* MOTHER *turns to* CORIE *and looks for help.*)

MOTHER. (*Frightened, grabs* CORIE'S *arm.*) What does
he mean by that?

CORIE. I don't know but I'm dying to find out. Will you
call me in the morning?

MOTHER. Yes . . . about six o'clock! (*And in a panic,
she exits.*)

CORIE. (*Takes a beat, closes the door, smiles and turns
to* PAUL.) Well . . . how about *that*, Mr. "This is going
to be a fiasco tonight"? . . . He's taking her all the way
out to New Jersey . . . at two o'clock in the morning
. . . That's what I call "The Complete Gentleman."
(PAUL *looks at her with disdain, rises and staggers up
the stairs into the bedroom.*) He hasn't even given a
thought about how he's going to get home . . . Maybe
he'll sleep over . . . Hey, Paul, do you think . . . ? No,
not *my* mother . . . (*Jumps up onto couch.*) Then again
anything can happen with the Sheik of Budapest . . .
Boy, what a night . . . Hey! I got a plan. Let's take the
bottle of scotch downstairs, ring all the bells and yell
"Police" . . . Just to see who comes out of whose apartment . . . (*There is no answer from the bedroom.*) Paul?
. . . What's the matter, darling . . . ? Don't you feel
well?

PAUL. (*Comes out of the bedroom, down the stairs,
crossing to the closet. He is taking his coat off and is*

angry.) What a rotten thing to do . . . To your own mother.

CORIE. What?

PAUL. Do you have any idea how she felt just now? Do you know kind of a night this was for her?

CORIE. (*Impishly.*) It's not over yet.

PAUL. You didn't see her sitting here two minutes ago. You were upstairs with that Hungarian Duncan Hines . . . Well, she was miserable. Her face was longer than that trip we took tonight. (*Hangs up coat in closet.*)

CORIE. She never said a thing to me.

PAUL. (*Takes out hanger and puts jacket on it.*) She's too good a sport. She went the whole cock-eyed way . . . Boy, oh boy . . . dragging a woman like that all the way out to the middle of the harbor for a bowl of sheep dip. (*Hangs jacket up and crosses to dictionary on side table under radiator. Takes tie off and folds it neatly.*)

CORIE. (*Follows him to table.*) It was Greek bean soup. And at least *she* tasted it. She didn't jab at it with her knife throwing cute little epigrams like, "Ho, ho, ho . . . I think there's someone in there."

PAUL. (*Puts tie between pages of dictionary.*) That's right. That's right. At least I was honest about it. You ate two bowls because you were showing off for Al Capone at the next table. (PAUL *searches for wallet unsuccessfully.*)

CORIE. What are you so angry about, Paul?

PAUL. (*Crossing to closet.*) I just told you. I felt terrible for your mother. (*Gets wallet out of jacket pocket.*)

CORIE. (*Following after him to the front of couch.*) Why? Where is she at this very minute? Alone with probably the most attractive man she's ever met. Don't tell me *that* doesn't beat hell out of hair curlers and the Late Late Show.

PAUL. (*Crossing up onto bedroom landing.*) Oh, I can just hear it now. What sparkling conversation. He's probably telling her about a chicken cacciatore he once cooked for the High Lama of Tibet and she's sitting there shoving pink pills in her mouth.

CORIE. (*Taking coat from couch and putting it on arm-chair* R.) You never can tell what people talk about when they're alone.

PAUL. I don't understand how you can be so unconcerned about this. (*Goes into bedroom.*)

CORIE. (*Moving to stairs.*) Unconcerned . . . I'm plenty concerned. Do you think I'm going to get one wink of sleep until that phone rings tomorrow? I'm scared to death for my mother. But I'm grateful there's finally the opportunity for something to be scared about . . . (*Moves* R., *then turns back.*) What I'm really concerned about is *you!*

PAUL. (*Bursts out of bedroom, nearly slamming through door.*) Me? Me?

CORIE. I'm beginning to wonder if you're capable of *having* a good time.

PAUL. Why? Because I like to wear my gloves in the winter?

CORIE. No. Because there isn't the least bit of adventure in you. Do you know what you are? You're a watcher. There are Watchers in this world and there are Do-ers. And the Watchers sit around watching the Do-ers do. Well, tonight you watched and I did.

PAUL. (*Moves down stairs to* CORIE.) Yeah . . . Well, it was harder to watch what you did than it was for you to *do* what I was watching. (*Crosses back up stairs to landing.*)

CORIE. You won't let your hair down for a minute. You couldn't even relax for one night. Boy, Paul, sometimes you act like a . . . a . . . (*Gets shoes from under couch.*)

PAUL. (*Stopping on landing.*) What . . . ? A stuffed shirt?

CORIE. (*Drops shoes on couch.*) I didn't say that.

PAUL. That's what you're implying.

CORIE. (*Moves to* R. *armchair and begins to take off jewelry.*) That's what you're anticipating. I didn't say you're a stuffed shirt. But you are extremely proper and dignified.

PAUL. I'm proper and dignified? (*Moves to* CORIE.) When . . . ? When was I proper and dignified?

CORIE. (*Turns to* PAUL.) All right. The other night. At Delfino's . . . You were drunk, right?

PAUL. Right. I was stoned.

CORIE. There you are. I didn't know it until you told me in the morning. (*Un-zips and takes off dress.*) You're a funny kind of drunk. You just sat there looking unhappy and watching your coat.

PAUL. I was watching my coat because I saw someone else watching my coat . . . Look, if you want, I'll get drunk for you sometime. I'll show you a slob, make your hair stand on end. (*Unbuttons shirt.*)

CORIE. (*Puts dress on chair.*) It isn't necessary.

PAUL. (*Starts to go, turns back.*) Do you know . . . Do you know, in P. J. Clarke's last New Year's Eve, I punched an old woman? . . . Don't tell me about drunks. (*Starts to go.*)

CORIE. (*Taking down hair.*) All right, Paul.

PAUL. (*Turns back and moves above couch.*) When else? When else was I proper and dignified?

CORIE. Always. You're always dressed right, you always look right, you always say the right things. You're very close to being perfect.

PAUL. (*Hurt to the quick.*) That's . . . that's a *rotten* thing to say.

CORIE. (*Moves up to* PAUL.) I have never seen you without a jacket. I always feel like such a slob compared to you. Before we were married I was sure you slept with a tie.

PAUL. No, no. Just for very *formal* sleeps.

CORIE. You can't even walk into a candy store and ask the lady for a Tootsie Roll. (*Playing the scene out, she moves* D. R. *of couch.*) You've got to walk up to the counter and point at it and say, "I'll have that thing in the brown and white wrapper."

PAUL. (*Moving to bedroom door.*) That's ridiculous.

CORIE. And you're not. That's just the trouble. (*Crosses to foot of stairs.*) Like Thursday night. You wouldn't walk barefoot with me in Washington Square Park. Why not?

PAUL. (*To head of stairs.*) Very simple answer. It was seventeen degrees.

CORIE. (*Back to chair and continues taking down hair.*) Exactly. That's very sensible and logical. Except it isn't any fun.

PAUL. (*Down stairs to couch.*) You know, maybe I *am* too proper and dignified for you. Maybe you would have been happier with someone a little more colorful and flamboyant . . . like the Geek! (*Starts back to bedroom.*)

CORIE. Well, he'd be a lot more laughs than a stuffed shirt.

PAUL. (*Turns back on landing.*) Oh, oh . . . I thought you said I wasn't.

CORIE. Well, you are now.

PAUL. (*Reflectively.*) I'm not going to listen to this . . . I'm not going to listen . . . (*Starts for bedroom.*) I've got a case in court in the morning.

CORIE. (*Moves* L.) Where are you going?

PAUL. To sleep.

CORIE. *Now?* How can you sleep now?

PAUL. (*Steps up on bed and turns back, leaning on door jamb.*) I'm going to close my eyes and count knichis. Good night!

CORIE. You can't go to sleep now. We're having a fight.

PAUL. *You* have the fight. When you're through, turn off the lights. (*Turns back into bedroom.*)

CORIE. Ooh, that gets me insane. You can even control your emotions.

PAUL. (*Storms out to head of stairs.*) Look, I'm just as upset as you are . . . (*Controls himself.*) But when I get hungry I eat. And when I get tired I sleep. You eat and sleep too. Don't deny it, I've seen you . . .

CORIE. (*Moves* R. *with a grand gesture.*) Not in the middle of a crisis.

PAUL. What crisis? We're just yelling a little.

CORIE. You don't consider this a crisis? Our whole marriage hangs in the balance.

PAUL. (*Sits on steps.*) It does? When did that happen?

CORIE. Just now. It's suddenly very clear that you and I have absolutely *nothing* in common.

PAUL. Why. Because I won't walk barefoot in the park in winter? You haven't got a case, Corie. Adultery, yes. Cold feet, no.

CORIE. (*Seething.*) Don't oversimplify this. I'm angry. Can't you see that?

PAUL. (*Brings his hands to his eyes and peers at her through imaginary binoculars. Then looks at his watch.*) Corie, it's two-fifteen. If I can fall asleep in about half-an-hour, I can get about five hours' sleep. I'll call you from court tomorrow and we can fight over the phone. (*Gets up and moves to bedroom.*)

CORIE. You will *not* go to sleep. You will stay here and fight to save our marriage.

PAUL. (*In doorway.*) If our marriage hinges on breathing fish balls and poofla-poo pie, it's not worth saving . . . I am now going to crawl into our tiny, little, single bed. If you care to join me, we will be sleeping from left to right tonight. (*Into bedroom and slams door.*)

CORIE. You won't discuss it . . . You're *afraid* to discuss it . . . I married a coward . . . ! (*Takes shoe from couch and throws it at bedroom door.*)

PAUL. (*Opens door.*) Corie, would you bring in a pail? The closet's dripping.

CORIE. Ohh, I hate you! I hate you! I really, really hate you!

PAUL. (*Storms to head of stairs.*) Corie, there is one thing I learned in court. Be careful when you're tired and angry. You might say something you will soon regret. I-am-now-tired-and-angry.

CORIE. And a coward.

PAUL. (*Comes down stairs to her at R. of couch.*) And I will now say something I will soon regret . . . Okay, Corie, maybe you're right. Maybe we have nothing in common. Maybe we rushed into this marriage a little too fast. Maybe Love isn't enough. Maybe two people should have to take more than a blood test. Maybe they should be checked for common sense, understanding and emotional maturity.

CORIE. (*That hurt.*) All right . . . Why don't you get it passed in the Supreme Court? Only those couples bearing a letter from their psychiatrists proving they're well adjusted will be permitted to be married.

PAUL. You're impossible.

CORIE. You're unbearable.

PAUL. You belong in a nursery school.

CORIE. It's a lot more fun than the Home for the Fuddy Duddies.

PAUL. (*Reaches out his hand to her.*) All right, Corie, let's not get—

CORIE. Don't you touch me . . . Don't you touch me . . . (PAUL *very deliberately reaches out and touches her.* CORIE *screams hysterically and runs across the room away from him. Hysterically.*) I don't want you near me. Ever again.

PAUL. (*Moves toward her.*) Now wait a minute, Corie—

CORIE. No. (*Turns away from him.*) I can't look at you. I can't even be in the same room with you now.

PAUL. Why?

CORIE. I just can't, that's all. Not when you feel this way.

PAUL. When I feel what way?

CORIE. The way you feel about me.

PAUL. Corie, you're hysterical.

CORIE. (*Even more hysterically.*) I am not hysterical. I know exactly what I'm saying. It's no good between us, Paul. It never will be again.

PAUL. (*Throwing up his hands and sinking to the couch.*) Holy cow.

CORIE. I'm sorry, I— (*She fights back tears.*) I don't want to cry.

PAUL. Oh, for pete's sakes, cry. Go ahead and cry.

CORIE. (*Height of fury.*) Don't you tell me when to

cry. I'll cry when I want to cry. And I'm not going to have my cry until you're out of this apartment.

PAUL. What do you mean, out of this apartment?

CORIE. Well, you certainly don't think we're going to live here together, do you? After tonight?

PAUL. Are you serious?

CORIE. Of course I'm serious. *I want a divorce!*

PAUL. (*Shocked, he jumps up.*) A *divorce?* What?

CORIE. (*Pulls herself together, and with great calm, begins to go up stairs.*) I'm sorry, Paul, I can't discuss it any more. Good night.

PAUL. Where are you going?

CORIE. To bed. (*Turns back to* PAUL.)

PAUL. You can't. Not now.

CORIE. You did before.

PAUL. That was in the middle of a fight. This is in the middle of a divorce.

CORIE. I can't talk to you when you're hysterical. Good night. (*Goes into bedroom.*)

PAUL. Will you come here . . . ? (CORIE *comes out on landing.*) I want to know why you want a divorce.

CORIE. I told you why. Because you and I have absolutely nothing in common.

PAUL. What about those six days at the Plaza?

CORIE. (*Sagely.*) Six days does not a week make.

PAUL. (*Taken aback.*) What does *that* mean?

CORIE. I don't know what it means. I just want a divorce.

PAUL. You know, I think you really mean it.

CORIE. I *do!*

PAUL. You mean, every time we have a little fight, you're going to want a divorce?

CORIE. (*Reassuring.*) There isn't going to be any more little fights. This is it, Paul! This is the end. Good night. (*Goes into bedroom and closes door behind her.*)

PAUL. Corie, do you mean to say—? (*He yells.*) Will you come down here!

CORIE. (*Yells from bedroom.*) Why?

PAUL. (*Screams back.*) Because I don't want to yeK.

(*The door opens and* CORIE *comes out. She stands at the top of the stairs. He points to his feet.*) All the way.

CORIE. (*Seething, comes all the way down and stands where he pointed.*) Afraid the crazy neighbors will hear us?

PAUL. You're serious.

CORIE. Dead serious.

PAUL. You mean the whole thing? With signing papers and going to court, shaking hands, goodbye, finished, fore-ever, divorced?

CORIE. (*Nodding in agreement.*) That's what I mean . . .

PAUL. I see . . . Well . . . I guess there's nothing left to be said.

CORIE. I guess not.

PAUL. Right . . . Well, er . . . Good night, Corie. (*And he goes up stairs.*)

CORIE. Where are you going?

PAUL. (*Turns back on landing.*) To bed.

CORIE. Don't you want to talk about it?

PAUL. At two-thirty in the morning?

CORIE. I can't sleep until this thing is settled. (*Moves to couch.*)

PAUL. Well, it may take three months. Why don't you at least take a *nap?*

CORIE. You don't have to get snippy.

PAUL. Well, dammit, I'm sorry, but when I plan vacations I'm happy and when I plan divorces I'm snippy. (*Crosses to bookcase and grabs attaché case.*) All right, you want to plan this thing, let's plan it. (*Storms to coffee table and sweeps everything there onto floor with his hand.*) You want a quick divorce or a slow painful one?

CORIE. (*Horrified.*) I'm going to bed. (*Goes up stairs.*)

PAUL. (*Shouts.*) You stay here or you get no divorce from me.

CORIE. (*Stops on landing.*) You can try acting civilized.

PAUL. (*Putting down attaché case.*) Okay, I'll be civilized. But charm you're not going to get. (*Pushes chair towards her.*) Now sit down! . . . Because there's a lot of legal and technical details to go through. (*Opening attaché case.*)

CORIE. Can't you do all that? I don't know anything about legal things.

PAUL. (*Wheels on her and in a great gesture points an accusing finger at her.*) Ah, haa . . . Now *I'm* the Do-er and *you're* the Watcher! (*Relentlessly.*) Right, Corie? Heh? Right? Right? Isn't that right, Corie?

CORIE. (*With utmost disdain.*) So this is what you're *really* like!

PAUL. (*Grimacing like the monster he is.*) Yes . . . Yes . . .

CORIE. (*Determined she's doing the right thing. She comes down stairs, and sits, first carefully moving the chair away from* PAUL.) All right, what do I have to do?

PAUL. First of all, what grounds? (*Sitting on couch.*)

CORIE. (*Not looking at* PAUL.) Grounds?

PAUL. (*Taking legal pad and pencil out of case.*) That's right. Grounds. What is your reason for divorcing me. And remember, my failure to appreciate knichis will only hold up in a Russian court.

CORIE. You're a scream, Paul. Why weren't you funny when we were happy?

PAUL. Okay . . . How about incompatible?

CORIE. Fine. Are you through with me?

PAUL. Not yet. What about the financial settlement?

CORIE. I don't want a thing.

PAUL. Oh, but you're entitled to it. Alimony, property? Supposing I just pay your rent. Seventy-five, sixty-three a month, isn't it?

CORIE. Ha ha—

PAUL. And you can have the furniture and the wedding gifts. I'd just like to keep my clothes.

CORIE. (*Shocked, she turns to* PAUL.) I hardly expected bitterness from you.

PAUL. I'm not bitter. That's a statement of fact. You're always wearing my pajamas and slippers.

CORIE. Only after you go to work.

PAUL. Why?

CORIE. Because I like the way they sm—never mind, it's stupid. (*She begins to sob, gets up and crosses up steps to bedroom.*) I'll sign over your pajamas and slippers.

PAUL. If you'd like, you can visit them once a month.

CORIE. (*Turns back on landing.*) *That's* bitter!

PAUL. You're damned right it is.

CORIE. (*Beginning to really cry.*) You have no right to be bitter.

PAUL. Don't tell me when to be bitter.

CORIE. Things just didn't work out.

PAUL. They sure as hell didn't.

CORIE. You can't say we didn't try.

PAUL. Almost two whole weeks.

CORIE. It's better than finding out in two *years*.

PAUL. Or twenty.

CORIE. Or fifty.

PAUL. Lucky, aren't we?

CORIE. We're the luckiest people in the whole world.

PAUL. I thought you weren't going to cry.

CORIE. Well, I am! I'm going to have the biggest cry I ever had in my life. And I'm going to enjoy it. (PAUL *drops pencil and pad into case, and buries his head in pillow from the couch.*) Because I'm going to cry so loud, I'm going to keep you awake all night long. Good night, Paul! . . . I mean, *goodbye!* (*She goes into bedroom and slams the door. We hear her crying in there.* PAUL *angrily slams his attaché case shut, gets up and moves towards stairs. At this moment, the bedroom door opens and* CORIE *throws out a blanket, sheet and pillow which land at* PAUL'S *feet. Then she slams the door shut again. Again we hear crying from the bedroom.* PAUL *picks them up and glares at door.*)

PAUL. (*Mimicking* CORIE.) All night long. (*Seething* PAUL *throws the bedding on the end table, and begins to try to make up the sofa with the sheet and blanket, all the while mumbling through the whole argument they have just had. As he puts the blanket over the sofa, he suddenly bursts out.*) Six days does not a week make.

(The PHONE rings. For a moment, PAUL *attempts to ignore it, but as it keeps on ringing, he finally storms over to it and rips the cord from the wall. Then, still mumbling to himself, he crosses to the light switch near the door and shuts off the LIGHTS. MOON-LIGHT from the skylight falls onto the sofa.* PAUL *gets into his makeshift bed and finally settles down.)* You work and work for a lousy six cents . . . *(And then it begins to snow. Through the hole in the sky-light it falls and down onto* PAUL'S *exposed head. He feels it, and after a quick moment, he rises up on his knees and looks up at the hole. Soundlessly, he crumples into a heap.)*

CURTAIN

ACT III

SCENE: *The following day. About 5 P.M.*

AT RISE: CORIE *is at the couch picking up the towels she has put down on the floor and the arm of the couch to soak up the water left by the previous night's snow. She picks up the towels with great distaste and uses one to rub off the arm. She looks up at the hole in the skylight, rolls the couch Downstage so that it will not be under the skylight, and takes the towels up into the bathroom. As she disappears into the bathroom, the front door opens and* PAUL *comes in, collapsing over the railing. He looks haggard and drawn, not just from the stairs, but from a lack of sleep and peace of mind. Also he has a cold, and as he leans there, he wearily blows his nose. He carries his attaché case and a newspaper. The DOORBELL buzzes, and as he presses the downstairs buzzer,* CORIE *comes out of the bathroom. They silently look at one another and then they* BOTH *move, wordlessly crossing each other;* PAUL *going up the steps to the bedroom and* CORIE *crossing up to the kitchen. Just before he gets to the bedroom door,* PAUL *sneezes.*

CORIE. (*About to go behind the screen, coldly, without looking at him.*) God bless him! (PAUL *goes into the bedroom and slams the door.* CORIE *goes into the kitchen. She comes out with two plates, two knives and forks and a napkin. Crossing to the table under the radiator, she puts down a plate with a knife and fork. Then putting the other setting down on the end table, she moves it all the way to the other side of the room,* D. R. *She goes back into the kitchen and emerges with two glasses. One she places on the side table and as she crosses towards the other table,* HARRY PEPPER, *our old friend, the* TELEPHONE

MAN, *appears at the door. He is breathing as hard as ever. She sees him.*) Oh, hi!

TELEPHONE MAN. (*Not too thrilled.*) Hello, again.

CORIE. How have you been?

TELEPHONE MAN. Fine. Fine, thanks.

CORIE. Good . . . The telephone's out of order.

TELEPHONE MAN. I know. I wouldn't be here for a social call.

CORIE. Come on in . . .

(*He steps up into apartment.* CORIE *closes the door behind him, and goes up into kitchen to fill her glass with water.*)

TELEPHONE MAN. (*Looking around.*) Hey! . . . Not bad . . . Not bad at all . . . You did a very nice job.

CORIE. (*Speaking from kitchen.*) Thanks. You know anyone who might want to rent it?

TELEPHONE MAN. You movin' *already?*

CORIE. (*Picking up salt and pepper shaker.*) I'm looking for a smaller place.

TELEPHONE MAN. (*Looks around with disbelief.*) Smaller than this? . . . They're not easy to find.

CORIE. (*Coming out of kitchen.*) I'll find one. (*Places glass of water and shakers on end table.*)

TELEPHONE MAN. (*Moves to phone.*) Well, let's see what the trouble is. (TELEPHONE MAN *picks up receiver, jiggles the buttons and listens.* CORIE *moves straight-back bentwood chair from* D. R. *to above the end table. Putting down receiver.*) It's dead.

CORIE. I know. My husband killed it. (*Crosses to side table under radiator, and takes candlestick and candle, and a small vase with a yellow rose.*)

TELEPHONE MAN. (*Puzzled.*) Oh! (*Looks down and notices the wire has been pulled from the wall. Kneels down, opens tool case, and cheerfully begins to replace the wire.*) So how do you like married life?

CORIE. (*Puts candlestick and vase down on her table; blandly.*) Very interesting. (*Goes up into kitchen.*)

TELEPHONE MAN. Well, after a couple of weeks, what's not interesting? Yeah, it's always nice to see two young kids getting started. With all the trouble today, you see a couple of newlyweds, you figure there's still hope for the world. (*As* CORIE *comes out of the kitchen with a pot of food, a ladle and a pot holder,* PAUL, *still in his overcoat and with his case and newspaper, comes out of the bedroom and slams the door behind him. Both* CORIE *and the* TELEPHONE MAN *stop.* PAUL *goes into the bathroom and slams that door hard.* CORIE *grimaces and the* TELEPHONE MAN *is shocked. Puzzled.*) Who's that?

CORIE. (*Rising above it.*) Him!

TELEPHONE MAN. Your husband?

CORIE. (*Crossing up to bathroom door.*) I suppose so. I wasn't looking. (*Pounds on the door with the ladle, and yells.*) Dinnah—is served! (*Crosses to side table and begins to ladle food onto plate.*)

(*The bathroom door opens.* PAUL *comes out.*)

PAUL. (*Nods at* TELEPHONE MAN *and then moves down stairs to the couch.*) I have my own dinner, thank you. (*Sits on couch, puts attaché case on table and opens it.*)

CORIE. (*Ignoring* PAUL, *crosses to* TELEPHONE MAN *and offers him plate.*) Would you like some goulash?

TELEPHONE MAN. (*Embarrassed, looks at* PAUL.) Er, no, thanks. We're not allowed to accept tips. (*He laughs at his small joke.* CORIE *takes the plate to kitchen and drops goulash, plate and all, into the garbage can. She then moves to her table and ladles goulash onto her plate.* PAUL, *in the meantime, has taken a small bag out of his attaché case. It contains a small bunch of grapes which he carefully places on top of his case.* CORIE *places the pot on the floor and, taking a book of matches from her apron pocket, lights the candle. While she does this she sings to herself . . . "Shama Shama . . ."* PAUL *buries himself in his paper and begins to eat his grapes. Taking all this in.*) I'll be out of here as fast as I can. (*Dives back to his work.*)

CORIE. (*Sitting down to eat.*) Take your time. No one's rushing you.

(*The* TELEPHONE MAN *begins a nervous, tuneless hum as he works.* PAUL *continues to eat and read wordlessly. There is a long pause.*)

PAUL. (*Without looking up.*) Is there any beer in the house? (CORIE *does not answer. The* TELEPHONE MAN *stops humming and looks at her, hoping she will. There is a pause,* PAUL *is still looking at his newspaper.*) I said, is there any beer in the house?

(*No answer.*)

TELEPHONE MAN. (*He can't stand it any longer*) Would you like me to look?

CORIE. There is *no* beer in the house.

(PAUL *throws down paper and storms toward* TELEPHONE MAN, *who draws back in fright.* PAUL *stops at bar and pours himself a drink.*)

TELEPHONE MAN. (*With great relief, and trying to make conversation because no one else will.*) That's *my* trouble . . . beer . . . I can drink ten cans in a night . . . of beer.

(PAUL *goes back to the couch and his newspaper. Not having eased the tension any, the* TELEPHONE MAN *goes back to his work and again begins his nervous humming.*)

PAUL. (*After another pause, still looking at his newspaper..*) Did my laundry come back today?

CORIE. (*With food in her mouth, takes her own sweet time in answering.*) Hmph.

PAUL. (*Looks at her.*) What does that mean?

CORIE. It meant your laundry came back today . . . They stuffed your shirts beautifully.

(Having watched this exchange, the TELEPHONE MAN *desperately begins to whistle a pointless and innocuous tune.)*

PAUL. *(Stung, takes a drink, then becoming aware of the* TELEPHONE MAN.) Would you like a drink? *(There is no answer. The* TELEPHONE MAN *continues to work.)* I said, would you like a drink?

TELEPHONE MAN. *(Startled, looks up from work.)* Who?

PAUL. You!

TELEPHONE MAN. Me?

PAUL. Yes!

TELEPHONE MAN. OH! . . . NO!

PAUL. Right. *(Goes back to his newspaper.)*

TELEPHONE MAN. *(Dives back to work.)* One more little screw should do it . . . There! *(Turns screw. Then says loud and elatedly.)* I'm finished! I'm finished! *(He throws tools quickly back into his kit.)* That wasn't too long, was it?

CORIE. No. Thank you very much.

TELEPHONE MAN. *(Getting up and crossing to door.)* It's A. T. & T.'s pleasure. *(Nearly drops kit, and in panic rushes to door. He is anxious to leave this scene.)*

CORIE. *(Picks up pot from floor and moves to him at door.)* I'm sorry to keep bothering you like this.

TELEPHONE MAN. Oh, listen. Anytime.

CORIE. *(Very confidingly.)* I don't think we'll be needing you again.

TELEPHONE MAN. Well, I wouldn't be too sure . . . Phones keep breaking down now and then but, er . . . *(He looks at* CORIE *as if trying to get some secret and personal message across to cheer her up.)* somehow, they have a way of getting fixed. You know what I mean . . . *(He winks at her to indicate, "Chins up." As he's winking,* PAUL *lowers his paper, turns around and sees him. The* TELEPHONE MAN *is terribly embarrassed. So he winks at* PAUL. *Then pulling himself together.)* Well . . . 'bye. *(And he rushes out of the door.)*

(CORIE *closes the door behind him and goes up into the*
kitchen with the pot and ladle. As soon as she is
safely behind the screen, PAUL *puts down his paper*
and runs to her table, where he swipes a mouthful
of goulash. Dashing to the couch, he is once more
hidden behind his newspaper and CORIE *comes out*
of the kitchen. She is now carrying a plate on which
rests a small, iced cake. She sits down, and pushing
her plate aside, begins to eat her cake.)

CORIE. Are you going to stay here again tonight?

PAUL. I haven't found a room yet.

CORIE. You've had all day to look.

PAUL. (*Using the nasal spray he had taken out of*
attaché case with the bag of grapes.) I've been very busy.
I work during the day, you know.

CORIE. You could look during your lunch hour.

PAUL. I *eat* during my lunch hour. I'll look during my
looking hour. (*Puts down spray and takes another drink.*)

CORIE. You could look tonight.

PAUL. I intended to. (*Goes back to reading paper.*)
But I'm coming down with a cold. I thought I'd just take
a couple of aspirins and get right into the sofa.

CORIE. I'm sure you can find *some* place . . . Why
don't you sleep at your club?

PAUL. It's not *that* kind of a club. It's a locker room
and a handball court . . . and to sleep there I'd have to
keep winning the serve. (*Looks at* CORIE.) Look, does it
bother you if I stay here another couple of days?

CORIE. It's your apartment too. Get out whenever you
want to get out. (*The PHONE rings. When* PAUL *makes*
no move to answer it, CORIE, *with great resignation,*
crosses to the phone and picks it up.) Hello? . . . Who?
. . . Yes, it is. (CORIE *suddenly acts very feminine, in*
a somewhat lower, more provocative and confidential
voice, even laughing at times as though she were sharing
some private little joke. She seems to be doing this all for
PAUL's *benefit. On phone.*) Oh, isn't that nice . . . Yes,
I'm very interested . . . (*Takes phone and moves away*

from PAUL.) Thursday night? . . . Well, I don't see why not . . .

PAUL. (*Doesn't like the sound of this.*) Who is that?

CORIE. (*Ignores him, laughs into phone.*) What's that? . . . Eight o'clock? . . . It sounds perfect.

PAUL. Who are you talking to?

CORIE. (*Still ignoring him.*) I see . . . But how did you get my number? . . . Oh, isn't that clever—

PAUL. (*Crosses angrily and grabs receiver.*) Give me that phone.

CORIE. (*Struggling with him for it.*) I will not. Get away from here, Paul. It's for me.

PAUL. I said give me that phone. (*Takes receiver and base of phone from her.* CORIE *storms across to her table with great indignation, blows candle out and begins to take her setting into kitchen. On phone.*) Hello? . . . Who is this? . . . Who? . . . (*Looks at* CORIE *incredulously.*) No, Madam, we're *not* interested in Bossa Nova lessons. (PAUL *hangs up and stares at* CORIE *as she comes out of kitchen.* CORIE *does not look at him as she finishes clearing the table and takes the plates into kitchen.* PAUL *moves back to the couch and sits.*) I'm glad we didn't have children . . . because you're a crazy lady.

CORIE. (*Moves chair back* D. R., *and carries table back to* R. *of couch.*) I'll go where I want and do what I want. And I'm not going to stay in this house at nights as long as you're here.

PAUL. (*Putting down paper.*) I see . . . Okay, Corie, when do you want me out?

CORIE. I want you out now. Tonight.

PAUL. (*Crossing to closet.*) Okay! Fine! (*He gets suitcase and puts it on top of end table.*) I'll be out of here in five minutes. Is that soon enough for you?

CORIE. Not if you can make it in two.

PAUL. (*Opening suitcase.*) You can't wait, can you? You just can't wait till I'm gone and out of your life.

CORIE. Right. When do I get it?

PAUL. Get what?

CORIE. My divorce. When do I get my divorce?

PAUL. How should I know? They didn't even send us our marriage license yet.

CORIE. I'll get your jockey shorts. (*Crosses up into bedroom.*)

PAUL. (*Moves to coffee table and takes drink.*) You can leave the suits. I'll pick them up in the spring when they're dry.

CORIE. (*In bedroom*) You'd better ring the bell. 'Cause I'm buying a big dog tomorrow.

PAUL. (*Finishing drink.*) A dog . . . Fine, fine . . . Now you'll have someone to walk barefoot in the park with. (*The PHONE rings. CORIE comes out of the bedroom with a pile of jockey shorts which she throws on the couch. She crosses to answer phone.*) If that's Arthur Murray, say hello. (*Gathers up jockey shorts and puts them in suitcase.*)

CORIE. (*Picks up phone.*) Hello . . . Yes, Aunt Harriet . . . What? . . . No, Mother's not with me . . . I'm positive . . . She left about two in the morning . . . What wrong? . . . *What?*

PAUL. (*Crossing to closet and getting pair of pants.*) What is it?

CORIE. (*Terribly frightened.*) Mother? . . . *My* Mother? . . . Are you *sure?*

PAUL. (*Putting pants in suitcase.*) What is it?

CORIE. (*Into phone, now very nervous.*) No, my phone's been out of order all day . . . (*Gives PAUL a dirty look.*) No, I don't know *what* could have happened.

PAUL. (*Blowing nose.*) What's the matter?

CORIE. All right, Aunt Harriet, don't get excited . . . Yes . . . Yes, I'll call as soon as I hear. (*She hangs up.*)

PAUL. (*Moves to CORIE.*) What happened to your mother?

CORIE. She didn't come home last night. Her bed wasn't slept in. Maybe I should call the police. (*Starts to pick up phone.*)

PAUL. All right, take it easy, Corie . . .

CORIE. (*Turns back to PAUL.*) Don't you understand?

Jessie looked. She was not in her bedroom this morning. (*Picks up phone.*)

PAUL. (*Groping.*) Well . . . well, maybe her back was bothering her and she went to sleep on the ironing board.

CORIE. You stupid idiot, didn't you hear what I said? My mother's been missing all night! . . . *My* mother!

PAUL. (*The Chief of Police.*) All right, let's not crack up.

CORIE. (*Seething.*) Will you go 'way? Get out of my life and go away! (*Slams receiver down and crosses to door.*) I don't want to see you here when I get back.

PAUL. Where are you going?

CORIE. Upstairs to find out what happened to my mother. (*She opens door.*) *And don't be here when I get back!* (*She goes out and slams the door.* PAUL *goes to door.*)

PAUL. Oh, yeah? . . . Well, I've got a big surprise for you . . . (*Opens door and yells after her.*) I'm not going to be here when you get back . . . (*Crossing to dictionary on side table.*) Let's see how you like living alone . . . (*Pulls ties out of dictionary and throws them in suitcase.*) A dog . . . Ha! That's a laugh . . . Wait till she tries to take him out for a walk . . . He'll get one look at those stairs and he'll go right for her throat. (*Crossing into bedroom.*) You might as well get a parakeet, too . . . So you can talk to him all night. (*Mimicking* CORIE.) "How much can I spend for bird seeds, Polly? Is a nickel too much?" (*Comes out of bedroom with shirts and pajamas.*) Well, fortunately, I don't need anyone to protect me. (*Putting clothes in suitcase.*) Because I am a man, sweetheart . . . An independent, mature, self-sufficient man. (*Sneezes as he closes suitcase.*) God bless me! (*Feeling sorry for himself, he feels his head.*) I probably got the flu. (*Crossing to bar, takes a bottle and glass.*) Yeah, I'm hot, cold, sweating, freezing. It's probably a 24-hour virus. I'll be all right . . . (*Looks at his watch.*) tomorrow at a quarter to five. (*Pours another drink, puts down bottle and drinks. As he drinks, he notices the hole in the skylight. Stepping up onto bluck leather armchair.*) Oh! . . . Oh, thanks a lot, pal. (*He holds glass up in toast fashion.*) "And thus it was written, some shall die by pestilence, some by the plague . . . and one poor schnook is gonna get it from a hole in the ceiling." (*Getting down, puts drink on side table.*) Well, I guess that's it. (*Gets bottle of scotch from bar. Glances at bedroom.*) Goodbye, leaky closet . . . (*To bathroom.*) Goodbye, no bathtub . . . (*Taking attaché case from coffee table, looks up at hole.*) Goodbye, hole . . . (*Getting suitcase.*) Goodbye, six flights . . . (*Starts for door. As* PAUL *moves to door,* CORIE *comes in. She holds her apron to her mouth, and is very disturbed.*) Goodbye, Corie . . . (PAUL *stops in the doorway as* CORIE *wordlessly goes right by him and starts to go up stairs to the bedroom.*) Don't I get a goodbye? . . According to law, I'm entitled to a goodbye!

CORIE. (*Stops on stairs and slowly turns back to* PAUL, *in a heart-rending wail.*) Goodbye . . . (*Goes into bedroom and collapses on the bed.*)

PAUL. Corie . . . Now what is it? (*Alarmed, he drops the suitcase, attaché case and puts the bottle on the endtable.*) Is it your mother? . . . Was it an accident? . . . (*Crosses to bedroom.*) Corie, for pete sakes, *what happened to your mother?* (*Suddenly* MOTHER *rushes in through the open door. She is now dressed in a man's bathrobe many sizes too big for her. Over-sized man's slippers flap on her bare feet. But she clutches her pocketbook. Desperately clutching the bathrobe, she crosses to the bedroom.*)

MOTHER. Corie, please, listen . . . ! It's not the way it looks at all!

PAUL. (*Looks at her in amazement.*) *Mother?*

MOTHER. (*Stops momentarily.*) Oh, good morning, Paul. (*Goes up stairs.*) Corie, you've got to talk to me. (CORIE *slams the door to the bedroom shut.*) There's a perfectly good explanation. (*Hysterical, in front of the closed door.*) Corie, please . . . You're not being fair . . . (*Turns to* PAUL.) Paul, make her believe me.

PAUL. (*Goes up stairs and pounds on bedroom door.*)

Now, you see . . . Now are you satisfied? . . . (*Turns to* MOTHER, *being very forgiving.*) It's all right, Mother, I understand. (*Starts for his suitcase.*)

MOTHER. (*Shocked.*) No . . . ! *You don't understand!* (*Goes to* PAUL.) You don't understand at all!

PAUL. (*Picking up suitcase, attaché case, and bottle.*) As long as you're all right, Mother. (*Looks at her, sadly shakes his head and exits.*)

MOTHER. (*Trying to stop him.*) No, Paul. . . . You've got to believe me. . . . (*But* PAUL *is gone.*) Oh, this is awful. . . . Somebody believe me.

(*The bedroom door opens and* CORIE *comes out.*)

CORIE. Paul! Where's Paul . . . ?

MOTHER. (*Putting bag down on end table.*) Corie, I'm going to explain everything. The bathrobe, the slippers. . . . It's all just a big mistake.

CORIE. (*Rushing to front door.*) Did he go? Did Paul leave?

MOTHER. (*Going to* CORIE.) It happened last night . . . when I left with Mr. Velasco. . . .

CORIE. (*Closing door.*) He was right. . . . Paul was right. (*Moves to couch and sits.*)

MOTHER. (*Following her.*) It must have been the drinks. I had a great deal to drink last night. . . . (*Sits next to* CORIE.) I had scotch, martinis, coffee, black bean soup and Uzus. . . .

CORIE. You don't have to explain a thing to me, Mother.

MOTHER. (*Horrified.*) But I want to explain. . . . When I got outside I suddenly felt dizzy . . . and I fainted. . . . Well, I passed out. In the slush.

CORIE. I should have listened to him. . . . It's all my fault.

MOTHER. (*Desperately trying to make her see.*) Then Victor picked me up and carried me inside. I couldn't walk because my shoes fell down the sewer.

CORIE. (*Deep in her own misery.*) You hear about these things every day.

MOTHER. He started to carry me up here but his beret fell over his eyes and he fell down the stairs. . . . He fell into Apartment 3C. I fell on his foot. . . . They had to carry us up.

CORIE. I thought we'd have a nice sociable evening, that's all.

MOTHER. Mr. Gonzales, Mr. Armandariz and Mr. Calhoun. . . . (*Sags in defeat.*) They carried us up. . . .

CORIE. Just some drinks, dinner and coffee. . . . That's all. . . .

MOTHER. And then they put us down. On the rugs. . . Oh, he doesn't have beds . . . just thick rugs, and then I fell asleep. . . .

CORIE. Paul was right. He was right about so many things. . . .

MOTHER. And then when I woke up, Victor was gone. But I was there . . . in his bathrobe. (*Pounds the couch with her fist.*) I swear that's the truth, Corie.

CORIE. (*Turns to* MOTHER.) You don't have to swear, Mother.

MOTHER. But I want you to believe me. I've told you everything.

CORIE. Then where are your clothes?

MOTHER. *That* I can't tell you.

CORIE. Why not?

MOTHER. Because you won't believe me.

CORIE. I'll believe you.

MOTHER. You won't.

CORIE. I will. Where are your clothes?

MOTHER. I don't know.

CORIE. I don't believe you. (*Gets up and moves towards her.*)

MOTHER. Didn't I say you wouldn't believe me? I just don't know where they are. . . . (*Gets up and moves* R.) Oh, Corie, I've never been so humiliated in all my life. . . .

CORIE. Don't blame yourself. . . . It's all my fault. *I* did it. I did this to you. (*Leans on bar, holding head.*)

MOTHER. And I had horrible nightmares. I dreamt my

fingers were falling off because I couldn't make a fist. (*Paces and catches sight of herself in mirror.*) Oh, God! I look like someone they woke up in the middle of the night on the Andrea Doria! (*Breaks into hysterical laughter.*)

(*There is a POUNDING on the door.*)

VELASCO'S VOICE. Hello. Anyone home?

MOTHER. (*Terror stricken.*) It's him. . . . (*Rushes to* CORIE.) Corie, don't let him in. I can't face him now. . . . Not in his bathrobe.

(*Another POUNDING at door.*)

VELASCO'S VOICE. Somebody, please!

CORIE. (*Moving past* MOTHER.) All right, Mother. I'll handle this. Go in the bedroom. . . .

MOTHER. (*Moving to stairs.*) Tell him I'm not here. Tell him anything.

(*The door opens and* VELASCO *steps in. He is now supporting himself with a cane and his foot is covered by a thick, white stocking. As* VELASCO *enters,* CORIE *sinks into the armchair,* R. *of the couch.*)

VELASCO. (*Hobbling up step and moving to couch.*) I'm sorry but I need some aspirins desperately. (VELASCO *catches sight of* MOTHER *who is furtively trying to escape up the stairs to the bedroom.*) Hello, Ethel.

MOTHER. (*Caught, stops and tries to cover her embarrassment.*) Oh, hello, Victor . . . Mr. Victor . . . Mr. Velasco.

VELASCO. (*To* CORIE.) Did you hear what happened to us last night? (*To* MOTHER.) Did you tell her what happened to us last night?

MOTHER. (*Horrified.*) Why . . . ? What happened to us last night? (*Composes herself.*) Oh, you mean what happened to us last night. (*With great nonchalance, moving down the stairs.*) Yes . . . Yes . . . I told her.

VELASCO. (*At couch.*) Did you know my big toe is broken?

MOTHER. (*Smiles.*) Yes. . . . (*Catches herself.*) I mean no. . . . Isn't that terrible?

VELASCO. I'll have to wear a slipper for the next month. . . . Only I can't find my slippers. . . . (*Sees them on* MOTHER's *feet.*) Oh, there they are. . . .

MOTHER. (*Looks down at her feet, as if surprised.*) Oh, yes. . . . There's your slippers.

VELASCO. (*Sitting on sofa and putting foot up on coffee table.*) It took me forty minutes to walk up the stairs. . . . I'll have to hire someone to pull me up the ladder. (*To* CORIE.) Corie, could I please have about three hundred aspirins? (CORIE *crosses to stairs.*)

MOTHER. (*Appealing to* CORIE.) A broken toe. . . . Isn't that awful! (CORIE *ignores her and goes into bathroom.*)

VELASCO. That's not the worst of it. I just had a complete examination. Guess what else I have?

MOTHER. What?

VELASCO. An ulcer! From all the rich food. . . . I have to take little pink pills like you.

MOTHER. Oh, dear. . . .

VELASCO. You know something, Ethel. . . . I don't think I'm as young as I think I am.

MOTHER. Why do you say that?

VELASCO. Isn't it obvious? Last night I couldn't carry you up the stairs. I can't eat rich foods any more . . . (*Very confidentially.*) and I dye my hair.

MOTHER. (*Moves to couch.*) Oh. . . . Well, it looks very nice.

VELASCO. Thank you. . . . So are you. . . .

MOTHER. (*Sitting next to* VELASCO.) Oh. . . . Thank you.

VELASCO. I mean it, Ethel. You're a very unusual woman.

MOTHER. Unusual . . . ? In what way?

VELASCO. (*Reflectively.*) It's funny, but I can hardly feel my big toe at all now.

MOTHER. (*Insistent.*) Unusual in what way?

VELASCO. Well, I took a look at you last night. . . . I took a long, close look at you. . . . Do you know what you are, Ethel?

MOTHER. (*Ready for the compliment.*) What?

VELASCO. A good sport.

MOTHER. Oh. . . . A good sport.

VELASCO. To have gone through all you did last night. The trip to Staten Island, the strange food, the drinks, being carried up to my apartment like that. And you didn't say one word about it.

MOTHER. Well, I didn't have much chance to . . . I did a lot of fainting.

VELASCO. Yes. . . . As a matter of fact, we both did. . . . If you remember. . . . (*Remembering, he begins to laugh.*)

MOTHER. Yes. . . . (*She joins in. It is a warm, hearty laugh shared by two friends. After the laugh gradually dies out, there is a moment of awkward silence and then with an attempt at renewed gaiety, MOTHER says:*) Mr. Velasco. . . . Where are my clothes?

VELASCO. Your clothes . . . .? Oh, yes. . . . (*Takes piece of paper out of pocket.*) Here. (*Gives it to her.*)

MOTHER. I'm sure I wore more than that.

VELASCO. It's a cleaning ticket. They're sending them up at six o'clock.

MOTHER. (*Taking ticket.*) Oh, they're at the cleaners. . . . (*After a moment's hesitation.*) When did I take them off?

VELASCO. You didn't. . . . You were drenched and out cold. Gonzales took them off.

MOTHER. (*Shocked.*) *Mr. Gonzales??*

VELASCO. Not Mister! . . . *Doctor* Gonzales!

MOTHER. (*Relieved.*) Doctor. . . . Oh, *Doctor* Gonzales. . . . Well, I suppose that's all right. How convenient to have an M.D. in the building.

VELASCO. (*Laughing.*) He's not an M.D. He's a Doctor of Philosophy.

MOTHER. (*Joins in laughter with great abandon.*) Oh, no. . . .

(CORIE *comes out of bathroom with aspirin and a glass of water. Watches them laughing with bewilderment.*)

CORIE. (*Crossing to above couch.*) Here's the aspirins.

VELASCO. Thank you, but I'm feeling better now.

MOTHER. *I'll* take them. (*Takes aspirin and sip of water.*)

VELASCO. (*Gets up and hobbles to door.*) I have to go. I'm supposed to soak my foot every hour. . . .

MOTHER. Oh, dear. . . . Is there anything I can do?

VELASCO. (*Turns back.*) Yes. . . . Yes, there is. . . . Would you like to have dinner with me tonight?

MOTHER. (*Surprised.*) Me?

VELASCO. (*Nods.*) If you don't mind eating plain food.

MOTHER. I love *plain* food.

VELASCO. Good. . . . I'll call the New York Hospital for a reservation. . . . (*Opens door.*) Pick me up in a few minutes. . . . We'll have a glass of buttermilk before we go. (*Exits.*)

MOTHER. (*After a moment, turns to* CORIE *on stairs and giggles. Takes grapes from coffee table.*) You know what . . . ? I'll bet I'm the first woman ever asked to dinner wearing a size 48 bathrobe.

CORIE. (*Lost in her own problem.*) Mother, can I talk to you for a minute?

MOTHER. (*Puts down bunch of grapes, gets up and moves* R.) I just realized. I slept without a board. . . . For the first time in years I slept without a board.

CORIE. Mother, will you listen—?

MOTHER. (*Turns to* CORIE.) You don't suppose Uzu is a Greek miracle drug, do you? (*Flips grape back and forth and pops it into her mouth like knichi.*)

CORIE. Mother, before you go, there's something we've got to talk about.

MOTHER. (*Moving to* CORIE.) Oh, Corie, how sweet.
. . . You're worried about me.

CORIE. I am *not* worried about you.

MOTHER. (*Looks in mirror.*) Oh, dear. My hair. What
am I going to do with my hair?

CORIE. I don't *care* what you do with your hair.

MOTHER. If *he* can dye it, why can't I? Do you think
black would make me look too Mexican?

CORIE. Mother, why won't you talk to me?

MOTHER. (*Moving* R. *above couch.*) Now . . . ? But
Victor's waiting. . . . (*Turns back to* CORIE.) Why
don't you and Paul come with us?

CORIE. That's what I've been trying to tell you. . . .
Paul isn't coming back.

MOTHER. What do you mean? Where'd he go?

CORIE. I don't know. Reno. Texas. Wherever it is that
men go to get divorced.

MOTHER. *Divorced?*

CORIE. That's right. Divorced. Paul and I have split
up. For good.

MOTHER. I don't believe it.

CORIE. Why don't you believe it?

MOTHER. You? And Paul?

CORIE. Well, you just saw him leave here with his suitcase. What did you think he had in there?

MOTHER. I don't know. I know how neat he is. I
thought maybe the garbage.

CORIE. Mother, I believe *you*. Why won't you believe
me?

MOTHER. (*Moving* L. *to bentwood armchair, sits fac-
ing* CORIE.) Because in my entire life I've never seen
two people more in love than you and Paul.

CORIE. (*Tearfully.*) Well, it's not true. It may have
been yesterday but it sure isn't today. It's all over,
Mother. He's gone.

MOTHER. You mean he just walked out? For no reason
at all . . . ?

CORIE. He had a perfectly *good* reason. I *told* him to
get out. *I* did it. Me and my big stupid mouth.

MOTHER. It couldn't have been all your fault.

CORIE. No . . . ? *No?* Because of me you're running around without your clothes and Paul is out there on the streets with a cold looking for a place to sleep. Whose fault is that?

MOTHER. Yours! . . . But do you want to know something that may shock you . . . ? I still love you.

CORIE. You do . . . ?

MOTHER. Yes, and Paul loves you too.

CORIE. And I love him. . . . Only I don't know what he wants. I don't know how to make him happy. . . . Oh, Mom, what am I going to do?

MOTHER. That's the first time you've asked my advice since you were ten. (*Gets up and moves to* CORIE.) It's very simple. You've just got to give up a little of you for him. Don't make everything a game. Just late at night in that little room upstairs. But take care of him. And make him feel important. And if you can do that, you'll have a happy and wonderful marriage. . . . Like two out of every ten couples. . . . But you'll be one of the two, baby. . . . (*Gently strokes* CORIE's *hair.*) Now get your coat and go on out after him. . . . I've got a date. (*Crosses to coffee table and picks up handbag.*) Aunt Harriet isn't going to believe a word of this. . . . (*Flourishing her bathrobe, moves to the door and opens it.*) I wish I had my Polaroid camera. . . . (*Pauses and blows* CORIE *a kiss and exits.*)

(CORIE *thinks a moment, wipes her eyes, and then rushes to the closet for her coat. Without stopping to put it on, she rushes to the door and opens it. As the door opens,* PAUL *is revealed at the doorway. He greets* CORIE *with a loud sneeze. His clothes are disheveled, his overcoat is gone, and he is obviously drunk, but he still is carrying his suitcase.*)

CORIE. Paul . . . ! Paul, are you all right . . . ?

PAUL. (*Very carefully crossing to the coffee table.*) Fine. . . Fine, thank you. . . . (*He giggles.*)

CORIE. (*Moves to him.*) I was just going out to look for you.

PAUL. (*Puts suitcase on floor and starts to take out clothes.*) Oh . . . ? Where were you going to look . . . ?

CORIE. I don't know. I was just going to look.

PAUL. (*Confidentially.*) Oh! . . . Well, you'll never find me. (*Throws a handful of clothes into the closet. He is apparently amused by some secret joke.*)

CORIE. Paul, I've got so much to say to you, darling.

PAUL. (*Taking more clothes out of suitcase.*) So have I, Corie. . . . I got all the way downstairs and suddenly it hit me. I saw everything clearly for the first time. (*Moves u. l. to above couch.*) I said to myself this is crazy. . . . Crazy . . . ! It's all wrong for me to run like this. . . . (*Turns to* CORIE.) And there's only one right thing to do, Corie.

CORIE. (*Moving to him.*) Really, Paul . . . ? What . . . ?

PAUL. (*Jubilantly.*) *You* get out! (*Breaks into hyssterical laughter.*)

CORIE. What . . . ?

PAUL. Why should I get out? I'm paying a hundred twenty-five a month . . . (*Looks about apartment.*) for this. . . . You get out. (*Stuffs clothes into dictionary.*)

CORIE. But I don't want to get out!

PAUL. (*Crossing back to suitcase and getting another handful of clothes.*) I'm afraid you'll have to. . . . The lease is in my name. . . . (*Moves to stairs.*) I'll give you ten minutes to pack your goulash.

CORIE. (*Moves to him.*) Paul, your coat! . . . Where is your coat?

PAUL. (*Draws himself up in indignation.*) Coat . . . ? I don't need a coat. . . . It's only two degrees. . . . (*Starts to go up stairs, slips and falls.*)

CORIE. (*Rushes to him.*) Paul, are you all right . . . ?

PAUL. (*Struggling up.*) You're dawdling, Corie. . . . I want you out of here in exactly ten minutes. . . .

CORIE. (*Holding him.*) Paul, you're ice cold. . . .
You're freezing . . . ! What have you been doing?

PAUL. (*Pulls away from her, moves to chair.*) What
do you think I've been doing? (*Puts his foot up on
seat.*) I've been walking barefoot in the goddam park.

CORIE. (*Pulls up his pants leg, revealing his stock-
ingless foot.*) Where's your socks . . . ? Are you crazy?

PAUL. No. . . . No. . . . But guess what I am.

CORIE. (*Looks at him.*) You're drunk!

PAUL. (*In great triumph, moves R.*) Ah . . . ! You
finally noticed!!

CORIE. Lousy, stinkin' drunk!

PAUL. Ah, gee. . . . Thanks. . . .

CORIE. (*Moves to him and feels his forehead*) You're
burning up with fever.

PAUL. How about that?

CORIE. You'll get pneumonia!

PAUL. If that's what you want, that's what I'll get.

CORIE. (*Leads him to couch.*) I want you to get those
shoes off. . . . They're soaking wet. . . . (*Pushes him
down onto couch.*)

PAUL. I can't. . . . My feet have swellened. . . .

CORIE. (*Pulling his shoes off.*) I never should have
let you out of here. I knew you had a cold. (*Puts shoes
on side table.*)

PAUL. (*Getting up and moving to doorway.*) Hey!
Hey, Corie. . . . Let's do that thing you said before.
. . . Let's wake up the police and see if all the rooms
come out of the crazy neighbors. . . . (*Opens door and
shouts into hall.*) All right, everybody up. . . .

CORIE. (*Runs to him and pulls him back into room.*)
Will you shut up and get into bed? (*As she struggles
with him, she tickles him, and PAUL falls to the floor
above couch. CORIE closes the door behind her.*) Get into
bed. . . .

PAUL. You get in first.

CORIE. You're sick.

PAUL. Not *that* sick. . . . (*He lunges for her and she
backs away against the door.*)

CORIE. Stop it, Paul. . . .

PAUL. Come on, Corie. Let's break my fever. . . . (*Grabs her.*)

CORIE. I said stop it! (*Struggling to get away.*) I mean it, damn you. . . . Stop it! (*Gives him an elbow in the stomach and dodges away through the kitchen.*)

PAUL. Gee, you're pretty when you're mean and rotten.

CORIE. Keep away from me, Paul. . . . (PAUL *moves towards her.*) I'm warning you. . . . I'll scream. (CORIE *keeps couch between her and* PAUL.)

PAUL. (*Stops.*) Shh . . . ! There's snow on the roof. We'll have an avalanche!

CORIE. (*Dodging behind chair.*) You shouldn't be walking around like this. You've got a fever. . . .

PAUL. (*Moving to chair.*) Stand still! The both of you!

CORIE. (*Running up stairs to bathroom.*) No, Paul . . . ! I don't like you when you're like this. (*Barricading herself in bathroom.*)

PAUL. (*Chasing her and pounding on door.*) Open this door!

CORIE. (*From bathroom.*) I can't. . . . I'm scared.

PAUL. Of me . . . ?

CORIE. Yes. . . .

PAUL. Why . . . ?

CORIE. Because it's not you any more. . . . I want the old Paul back.

PAUL. That faddy duddy?

CORIE. He's not a fuddy duddy. He's dependable and he's strong and he takes care of me and tells me how much I can spend and protects me from people like you. . . . (PAUL *suddenly arrives at a brainstorm and with great glee sneaks off into the bedroom.*) And I just want him to know how much I love him. . . . And that I'm going to make everything here exactly the way he wants it. . . . I'm going to fix the hole in the skylight . . . and the leak in the closet. . . . And I'm going to put in a bathtub and if he wants I'll even carry him up the stairs every night . . . Because I want him to know how much I love him. . . . (*Slowly and cautiously opening door.*) Can you hear me, darling . . . ? Paul? . . . (PAUL *appears on the skylight. He is crawling, drunkenly, along the ledge.* CORIE, *having gotten no answer, comes out of the bathroom and goes into the bedroom searching for* PAUL.) Paul, are you all right? (*Comes out of bedroom and crosses towards front door. When she is beneath him,* PAUL *taps on the skylight and stands up.* CORIE, *looking up, sees him and screams.*) Paul! . . . You   idiot. . . . Come   down. . . . You'll kill yourself.

PAUL. (*Teetering on ledge, yelling through skylight.*) I want to be a nut like everyone else in this building.

CORIE. (*Up on her knees on couch, yelling back.*) No! No, Paul . . . ! I don't want you to be a nut. I want you to come down.

PAUL. I'll come down when you've said it again. . . . Loud and clear.

CORIE. What . . . ? Anything, Paul. . . . Anything!

PAUL. "My husband . . ."

CORIE. 'My husband . . .'

PAUL. "Paul Bratter . . ."

CORIE. 'Paul Bratter . . .'

PAUL. ". . . rising young attorney . . ." (*Nearly falls off ledge.*)

CORIE. (*Screaming in fright.*) '. . . rising young attorney . . .'

PAUL. ". . . is a lousy stinkin' drunk . . ."

CORIE. '. . . is a lousy stinkin' drunk.' . . . And I love him.

PAUL. And I love you, Corie. Even when I didn't like you, I loved you.

CORIE. (*Crossing to* PAUL.) Then please, darling. . . . Please, come down.

PAUL. I . . . I can't. . . . Not now.

CORIE. Why not?

PAUL. I'm going to be sick. . . . (*Looking around as if to find a place to be sick.*)

CORIE. Oh, no!

PAUL. Oh, yes!

CORIE. (*Paces back and forth.*) Paul. . . . Paul. . . . Don't move! I'll come out and get you.

PAUL. (*Holding on desperately.*) Would you do that, Corie? Because I'm getting panicky!

CORIE. Yes. . . . Yes, darling, I'm coming. . . . (*Runs off into bedroom.*)

PAUL. Corie. . . . Corie. . . .

CORIE. (*Dashing out of bedroom and down stairs.*) What, Paul . . . ? What?

PAUL. Don't leave me. . . .

CORIE. You'll be all right, darling. Just hold on tight. And try to be calm. . . .

PAUL. How . . . ? What should I do?

CORIE. (*Ponders.*) What should he do . . . ? (*To* PAUL.) Sing, Paul!

PAUL. Sing . . . ?

CORIE. Sing. . . . Keep singing as loud as you can until I come out there. Promise me you'll keep singing, Paul. . . .

PAUL. Yes, yes. . . . I promise. . . . I'll keep singing. . . .

CORIE. (*Moving to stairs.*) But don't stop until I come out. . . . I love you, darling. . . . Keep singing, Paul. . . . Keep singing! (*Runs off into bedroom.*)

PAUL. (*Calling after her in desperation.*) Corie, Corie, what song should I sing? . . . Oh, God. . . . (*Pulls himself together.*) "Shama shama . . ."

CURTAIN

PROPERTY PLOT

ACT ONE

On Stage:
6 foot wooden ladder, locked open U. L. C.
Empty, five gallon paint bucket, upside down, R. of ladder
Small, spattered canvas drip cloth—over paint bucket
Small, empty paint can—on top of canvas on bucket
Iron stove with opened doors—D. L.

On stove—box of small wooden matches
Old gas range—U. L. in kitchen

On range: wadded newspapers
Chipped sink with running water—C. in kitchen
Old refrigerator—D. S. in kitchen

On refrigerator: wadded newspapers
Steam riser pipe—D. R.

On pipe: old rag
Raised radiator on shelf—U. L. C.

On pipe to radiator: old rag
Bookcase—L. of kitchen platform

On Platform U. R. C.:
Closed steamer trunk—U. R. of platform, angled U. R. to D. L.
on end
Small blue suitcase—L. of steamer, U. and D. S.

In small suitcase: new black nightgown, assorted lingerie
Medium size, blue suitcase—R. of small case, angled D. R. to
U. L.

In medium suitcase: bottle of champagne, 4 wooden legs
Large, grey suitcase—L. of medium suitcase, angled U. R.—
D. L.
Small, blue make-up case—D. R. of grey suitcase

In Bathroom U. L. C.:
Shower R.—shower curtain
Pedestal sink with mirror—L. of shower
Towel rack—gold towel

94

Over Platform D. L.:
  Naked light bulb in fixture

On right of downstage wall of D. L. *platform:* telephone box

On Prop Table Off Stage Right:
  Wrapped bouquet of yellow and red mums (Corie)
  Black tool kit bag (Telephone Man)
  Beige princess phone with 15 foot cord (Telephone Man)
  Order book (Telephone Man)
  Work belt with screwdriver, etc. (Telephone Man)
  Large, wrapped package from Lord & Taylor with blanket
    (Delivery Man)
  Medium wrapped package from Lord & Taylor with dis-
    mantled coffee pot (Delivery Man)
  Smaller wrapped package from Lord & Taylor with clock and
    broken materials (Delivery Man)
  Receipt book and pencil (Delivery Man)
  Black attache case with legal papers, affidavits, legal pads
    and pencils (Paul)
  Large grey Samsonite suitcase (Paul)
  Brown paper bag with bottle of Vat 69 (Paul)
  Pocketbook (Mother)

Off Right—Door Slam

Check List:
  Bedroom door closed—bathroom door slightly open
  Ladder locked in position and sturdy
  Water set for faucet
  Light bulb set in fixture
  Cigarettes and matches in Corie's coat
  All doors opened
  Bed struck from bedroom
  Drape struck from closet
  Shower curtain struck from shower
  Refrigerator cleared
  Snow bag filled and rigged
  Corie's purse to off R.

ACT TWO

Furniture on Stage:
  Straight bentwood chair with red cushion D. R.
  Carved back armchair with red cushion D. R. C.
  Upholstered wrought iron sofa—Center, angled D. R.—U. L.

On sofa:
    Right—maroon and gold pillows
    Left—print and brown pillows
Carved wood coffee table—D. S. of sofa, D. R.—U. L.

On coffee table:
    Wooden canape tray L.
    Ashtray, cigarettes, lighter and matches—C.
Bentwood armchair with black leather seat—D. L. of sofa
Bamboo open bar—D. of bedroom platform

On bar:
    Top—
        Weather vane R.
        Decanter with Scotch
        Decanter with whiskey
        Lamps with green shades
        Beige telephone
        Martini shaker with stirrer
        4 highball glasses
    Bottom shelf—
        Brass ashtray
        Brass cannon
        1 decanter
        Scotch bottle
        2 Cognac bottles
        4 old fashioned glasses
Straight bentwood chair with red cushion D. L.
Bamboo screen—L. on kitchen platform
Perspective breakfront—right on U. R. C. platform

On breakfront: glass bell
Small bentwood rocking chair—U. C. on U. R. C. platform
Light wood, Spanish desk—U. L. C.

On desk: hurricane lamp, brass engine, plant with green
    vase
Bentwood end table with green felt cover—R. of sofa
Straight cane chair with red cushion—D. S. of desk
Dark, carved side table—L. C. under radiator

On side table:
    Wooden figure lamp with red shade U. S.
    Bud vase with rose
    Brass candlestick with candle
    Large dictionary with folded ties
    Small bust

Over side table:
Gold framed mirror
Bentwood planter with mirror—on D. L. platform L. of bathroom

On planter:
Pitcher on bottom, bowl with plant on top
Brush, comb and bobby pins R. shelf
Ear rings L. shelf

Props and Dressing:
Austrian Screen over skylight—up position
Brown striped drapery over closet D. R.

In closet:
2 coats (dressing)
1 pants on hanger
Blazer with wallet in pocket (Paul)
3 wooden hangers
White figured wool rug—on floor C. S.

In kitchen:
In refrigerator—
Strike champagne bottle and paper
Dress with food

On drain:
Ice bucket empty with top taped on (on stove)
4 cups and saucers
1 bottle of Maxwell House instant coffee (on stove)
4 spoons

On stove:
One sauce pan for water
Coffee pot
Empty garbage pail—D. L. of screen (wax bag in can)
2 plants—D. R. of screen

On U. R. C. Platform:
3 pillows—U. L.

Over windows U. C.:
White curtains with black band

Over door:
Ship—bas relief

Pictures:
3—U. S. of kitchen

1—R. of U. S. windows
In bedroom—U. S.
1—over closet

In bedroom:
Made up bed
Blue blanket, blue and white sheet and pillow (Corie)
Blue and red striped tie (Paul)
Black evening coat (Corie)
Black bag (Corie)
Blue muffler (Paul)

In bathroom:
Shower curtain
Towels on towel rack

Over D. L. *Platform:*
Green shade on fixture

Strike:
Clock
Steamer trunk
Rags from pipes
Flowers in paint can
Wood from stove
Paper from refrigerator and stove
Box with blanket
Ladder
Champagne bottle and paper from refrigerator
Corie's purse
Rags from pipes R. and L.
Clock from Refrigerator

RE-SET:
Phone to bar, logs struck D. S. of stove, suitcase in closet

Off right:
Brown paper bag with Gilbys & Beefeater's Gin
(Corie)
Box with canapes (Corie)
Pocket book with bottle of pink pills (Mother)
Casserole with knichis and wad of bubble gum
(Velasco)
Asbestos cooking glove—L. (Velasco)
Handkerchief (Velasco)
Four small brandy glasses (Velasco)
Attache case (Paul)

Check:

Keys off R. (Corie)
Garbage pail—empty
Dictionary D. S. on side table
Shade on fixture D. L.
Lamps plugged and working
Snow bag rigged
Pink pills in Mother's handbag
Attache case for Paul
Corie's black coat and bag in bedroom
Blue suitcase L. in closet
Phone to bar
Rigging for phone to be pulled out
All doors closed
Prop man for scene change
Wristwatch for Paul
Wristwatch for Velasco

Between Act II—Scene 1 and Act II—Scene 2:

Strike:

Martini pitcher—empty 3 glasses into pitcher
Props—move carved back armchair R. one foot, move sofa
U. S.

ACT THREE

RE-SET:

Straight bentwood chair with red cushion L. of R. portal
Bentwood end table with green felt cover—L.
Upholstered wrought iron sofa—angled upstage
Carved wood coffee table—D. S. parallel to curtain
Bentwood armchair with black leather seat—angled U. S.
Frame for Austrian curtain on skylight—smaller
Dictionary on side table moves upstage

Strike:

No. 1 skylight drape

Set:

Short skylight drape

Strike:

From coffee table—
Canapes and tray
Lighter, cigarette holder, ashtray and matches
Martini mixer, 2 bottles of gin, 3 martini glasses, ice bucket

Re-Set:
   Black attache case off R. with pencil, nasal spray, pill bottles
   and bag of grapes

Strike:
   From couch—
      Blanket, chest, pillow case and pillow
   From desk—
      Knichi pot and cover and knichis
   From side table—
      Strike martini glass
   From book case—
      Knichi pot cover
   From bar—
      Re-set brandy decanter in shelf
      Re-set phone on bar
      Re-set decanters L. on bar
      Re-set 4 plastic glasses
   From closet—
      Re-set black overcoat (Paul) off R.
   From skylight—
      Strike large shade
   From kitchen—
      Strike cups, saucers and spoons
      Strike pot and Maxwell House Coffee

Set:
   Two rust towels D. L. of sofa
   One white towel over L. arm of sofa

   In kitchen:
      On drain—
         2 plates with 2 knives, 2 forks, and 1 gold napkin
         1 crystal glass, 1 plain glass
         1 jelly glass
         Crystal salt and pepper shakers
         Small plate with small cake
         Bag and box from garbage can
      On stove—
         Sauce pan with goulash
         Ladle
         Pot holder
         Cake
         Box of matches

On skylight:
  Small shade
  On bar—
    R. of top shelf—bottle of Scotch (R. of weathervane)
    D. R.—4 highball glasses (R. of weathervane)

In bathroom:
  Glass of water (Corie)

On coffee table:

In closet:
  Black and white check apron with matches in pocket
    (Corie)
  Fur coat (Corie's), suitcase

Off Left in bedroom:
  Jockey shorts (Corie)
  T-shirts (Corie)
  White dress shirts (Paul)
  Pair of pajamas (Paul)

Off Stage Right:
  Black work bag (Telephone Man)
  New York Times (Paul)
  Black cane (Velasco)
  Dry cleaning slip (Velasco)
  1 handkerchief (Paul)
  Black attache case off R.

Check List:
  Change of frame on skylight
  Black overcoat off R.
  Grey jacket and blazer off R.
  Black attache case off R. with grapes, pills and nasal spray
  Dictionary U. S. on side table
  Shaggy fur coat in closet
  Blue suitcase in closet
  Garbage can empty
  Check front of stage
  Paul's overcoat, grey jacket and blazer from closet to off R.
  Small Austrian shade on skylight
  Stoppers loose in decanters

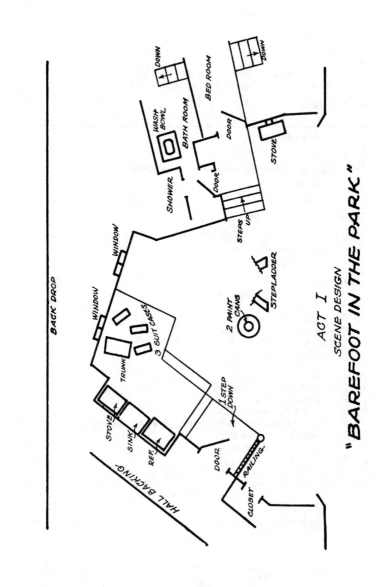

ACT I

SCENE DESIGN

"BAREFOOT IN THE PARK"

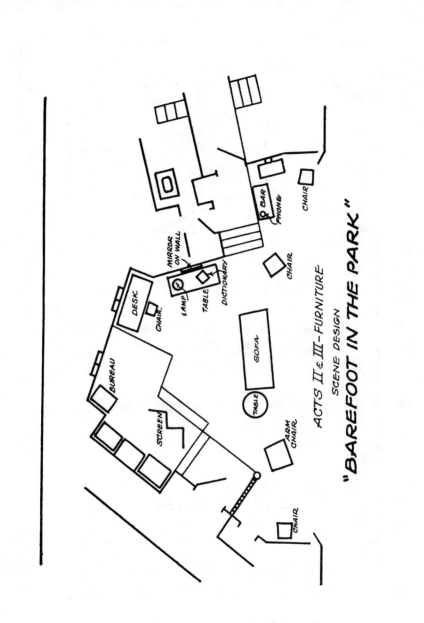

ACTS II & III – FURNITURE

SCENE DESIGN

"BAREFOOT IN THE PARK"